WELCOME TO
ROBERT SILVERBERG'S WORLDS

You'll visit one world in which Germany won World War I; another in which the inhabitants of other planets regard Earth people as simple, charming and harmless; yet another, in which men and women regularly change bodies. And you'll meet some of his characters: A crab-like alien who is fashionable with Lower Manhattan's artists; a giant bat who visits Earth to pledge eternal friendship for the human race; and a robot cook who will go to *any* lengths to ensure that his masters lose weight.

When you come back to reality, you will have learned why Silverberg is one of the premier sf writers of our time...

ROBERT SILVERBERG

NEEDLE IN A TIME STACK

ACE SCIENCE FICTION BOOKS
NEW YORK

ACKNOWLEDGMENTS

*The Iron Chancellor copyright © Galaxy Publishing Company 1958
The Reality Trip copyright © Universal Publishing & Distributing
Corporation 1970
The Shrines of Earth copyright © Street & Smith Publications, Inc. 1957
Black is Beautiful copyright © Harry Harrison 1970
Ringing the Changes copyright © Anne McCaffrey 1970
Translation Error copyright © Street & Smith Publications, Inc. 1959
*The Shadow of Wings copyright © Galaxy Publishing Company 1963
*Absolutely Inflexible copyright © King-Size Publications, Inc. 1956
*His Brother's Weeper copyright © King-Size Publications, Inc. 1959
*These stories were included in the original edition of NEEDLE IN A TIMESTACK

NEEDLE IN A TIMESTACK

An Ace Science Fiction Book/published by arrangement with
the author

PRINTING HISTORY
Ballantine edition/November 1966
Sphere edition/1967
Revised Sphere edition/1979
Ace Science Fiction edition/November 1985

ISBN: 0-441-56872-6

Ace Science Fiction Books are published by
The Berkley Publishing Group,
200 Madison Avenue, New York, New York 10016.
PRINTED IN THE UNITED STATES OF AMERICA

PREFACE TO THE SECOND EDITION

"Oh, sir, things change," says one of the characters in my story *Born With the Dead*, and one place where that seems to be true is the publishing industry. Books go in and out of print, reappear in unexpected places with new covers and transmogrified interiors, and—sometimes—even change their contents. As herewith. My collection of stories, NEEDLE IN A TIME-STACK, first appeared in the United States in 1966, a year later in Great Britain. In the interim the book has vanished several times, surfacing each time in a new and shinier format; but during the periods of vanishment, I have on occasion blithely borrowed stories from the collection to use in *other* collections, thinking that in the eternal Heraclitean flow of things it wouldn't make much difference. Perhaps it doesn't make much difference to most people, but it has begun to matter to me, and, as my various short story collections undergo their latest set of incarnations I am going to some pains to eliminate all such duplications and overlaps of material.

So what we have here is NEEDLE IN A TIME-STACK, but not quite the same book that was published under that title a decade and more ago. About half of the original stories have been retained; the other stories, subsequently made available in other books, have been erased here and replaced with a group of stories of about the same length, vintage, and quality that are *not* (I hope) available in any other collection of mine. It is a ploy calculated to drive bibliographers insane, but should not interfere with the pleasures of normal readers.

Robert Silverberg
October, 1977

CONTENTS

THE IRON CHANCELLOR

The Carmichaels were a pretty plump family, to begin with. Not one of the four of them couldn't stand to shed quite a few pounds. And there happened to be a superspecial on roboservitors at one of the Miracle Mile roboshops—40% off on the 2061 model, with adjustable caloric-intake monitors.

Sam Carmichael liked the idea of having his food prepared and served by a robot who would keep one beady solenoid eye on the collective family waistline. He squinted speculatively at the glossy display model, absentmindedly slipped his thumbs beneath his elastobelt to knead his paunch, and said, "How much?"

The salesman flashed a brilliant and probably synthetic grin. "Only 2995, sir. That includes free service contract for the first five years. Only two hundred credits down and up to forty months to pay."

Carmichael frowned, thinking of his bank balance. Then he thought of his wife's figure, and of his daughter's endless yammering about her need to diet. Besides, Jem-

1

ima, their old robocook, was shabby and gear-stripped, and made a miserable showing when other company executives visited them for dinner.

"I'll take it," he said.

"Care to trade in your old robocook, sir? Liberal trade-in allowances—"

"I have a '43 Madison." Carmichael wondered if he should mention its bad arm libration and serious fuel-feed overflow, but decided that would be carrying candidness too far.

"Well—ah—I guess we could allow you fifty credits on a '43, sir. Seventy-five, maybe, if the recipe bank is still in good condition."

"Excellent condition." That part was honest—the family had never let even one recipe wear out. "You could send a man down to look her over."

"Oh, no need to do that, sir. We'll take your word. Seventy-five, then? And delivery of the new model by this evening?"

"Done," Carmichael said. He was glad to get the pathetic old '43 out of the house at any cost.

He signed the purchase order cheerfully, pocketed the facsim and handed over ten crisp twenty-credit vouchers. He could almost feel the roll of fat melting from him now, as he eyed the magnificent '61 roboservitor that would shortly be his.

The time was only 1810 hours when he left the shop, got into his car and punched out the coordinates for home. The whole transaction had taken less than ten minutes. Carmichael, a second-level executive at Normandy Trust, prided himself both on his good business sense and his ability to come quickly to a firm decision.

Fifteen minutes later, his car deposited him at the front entrance to their totally detached self-powered suburban home in the fashionable Westley subdivision. The car obediently took itself around back to the garage, while Carmichael stood in the scanner field until the door opened. Clyde, the robutler, came scuttling hastily up, took his hat and cloak, and handed him a Martini.

Carmichael beamed appreciatively. "Well done, thou good and faithful servant!"

He took a healthy sip and headed toward the living room to greet his wife, son and daughter. Pleasant gin-induced warmth filtered through him. The robutler was ancient and due for replacement as soon as the budget could stand the charge, but Carmichael realized he would miss the clanking old heap.

"You're late, dear," Ethel Carmichael said as he appeared. "Dinner's been ready for ten minutes. Jemima's so annoyed her cathodes are clicking."

"Jemima's cathodes fail to interest me," Carmichael said evenly. "Good evening, dear. Myra. Joey. I'm late because I stopped off at Marhew's on my way home."

His son blinked. "The robot place, Dad?"

"Precisely. I bought a '61 roboservitor to replace old Jemima and her spluttering cathodes. The new model has," Carmichael added, eyeing his son's adolescent bulkiness and the rather-more-than-ample figures of his wife and daughter, "some very special attachments."

They dined well that night, on Jemima's favorite Tuesday dinner menu—shrimp cocktail, fumet of gumbo chervil, breast of chicken with creamed potatoes and asparagus, delicious plum tarts for dessert, and coffee. Carmichael felt pleasantly bloated when he had finished, and gestured to Clyde for a snifter of his favorite after-dinner digestive aid, VSOP Cognac. He leaned back, warm, replete, able easily to ignore the blustery November winds outside.

A pleasing electroluminescence suffused the dining room with pink—this year, the experts thought pink improved digestion—and the heating filaments embedded in the wall glowed cozily as they delivered the BTUs. This was the hour for relaxation in the Carmichael household.

"Dad," Joey began hesitantly, "about that canoe trip next weekend—"

Carmichael folded his hands across his stomach and nodded. "You can go, I suppose. Only be careful. If I find out you didn't use the equilibriator this time—"

The door chime sounded. Carmichael lifted an eyebrow and swivelled in his chair.

"Who is it, Clyde?"

"He gives his name as Robinson, sir. Of Robinson Robotics, he said. He has a bulky package to deliver."

"It must be that new robocook, Father!" Myra Carmichael exclaimed.

"I guess it is. Show him in, Clyde."

Robinson turned out to be a red-faced, efficient-looking little man in greasy green overalls and a plaid pullover-coat, who looked disapprovingly at the robutler and strode into the Carmichael living room.

He was followed by a lumbering object about seven feet high, mounted on a pair of rolltreads and swathed completely in quilted rags.

"Got him all wrapped up against the cold, Mr. Carmichael. Lot of delicate circuitry in that job. You ought to be proud of him."

"Clyde, help Mr. Robinson unpack the new robocook," Carmichael said.

"That's okay—I can manage it. And it's *not* a robocook, by the way. It's called a roboservitor now. Fancy price, fancy name."

Carmichael heard his wife mutter, "Sam, how much—"

He scowled at her. "Very reasonable, Ethel. Don't worry so much."

He stepped back to admire the roboservitor as it emerged from the quilted swaddling. It was big, all right, with a massive barrel of a chest—robotic controls are always housed in the chest, not in the relatively tiny head—and a gleaming mirror-keen finish that accented its sleekness and newness. Carmichael felt the satisfying glow of pride in ownership. Somehow it seemed to him that he had done something noble and lordly in buying this magnificent robot.

Robinson finished the unpacking job and, standing on tiptoes, opened the robot's chest panel. He unclipped a thick instruction manual and handed it to Carmichael, who stared at the tome uneasily.

"Don't fret about that, Mr. Carmichael. This robot's no trouble to handle. The book's just part of the trimming. Come here a minute."

Carmichael peered into the robot's innards. Pointing, Robinson said, "Here's the recipe bank—biggest, and best ever designed. Of course it's possible to tape in any of your favorite family recipes, if they're not already there. Just hook up your old robocook to the integrator circuit and feed 'em in. I'll take care of that before I leave."

"And what about the—ah—special features?"

"The reducing monitors, you mean? Right over here. See? You just tape in the names of the members of the family and their present and desired weights, and the roboservitor takes care of the rest. Computes caloric intake, adjusts menus, and everything else."

Carmichael grinned at his wife. "Told you I was going to do something about our weight, Ethel. No more dieting for you, Myra—the robot does all the work." Catching a sour look on his son's face, he added, "And you're not so lean yourself, Buster."

"I don't think there'll be any trouble," Robinson said buoyantly. "But if there is, just buzz for me. I handle service and delivery for Marhew Stores in this area."

"Right."

"Now if you'll get me your obsolete robocook, I'll transfer the family recipes before I cart it away on the trade-in-deal."

There was a momentary tingle of nostalgia and regret when Robinson left, half an hour later, taking old Jemima with him. Carmichael had almost come to think of the battered '43 Madison as a member of the family. After all, he had bought her sixteen years before, only a couple of years after his marriage.

But she—*it*, he corrected in annoyance—was only a robot, and robots became obsolete. Besides, Jemima probably suffered all the aches and pains of a robot's old age and would be happier dismantled. Carmichael blotted Jemima from his mind.

The four of them spent most of the rest of that evening discovering things about their new roboservitor. Carmichael drew up a table of their weights (himself, 192; Ethel, 145; Myra, 139; Joey, 189) and the amount they proposed to weigh in three months' time (himself, 180; Ethel, 125; Myra, 120; Joey, 175). Carmichael then let his son, who prided himself on his knowledge of practical robotics, integrate the figures and feed them to the robot's programming bank.

"You wish this schedule to take effect immediately?" the roboservitor queried in a deep, mellow bass.

Startled, Carmichael said, "T-tomorrow morning, at breakfast. We might as well start right away."

"He speaks well, doesn't he?" Ethel asked.

"He sure does," Joey said. "Jemima always stammered and squeaked, and all she could say was, 'Dinner is serrved' and 'Be careful, sirr, the soup plate is verry warrm.'"

Carmichael smiled. He noticed his daughter admiring the robot's bulky frame and sleek bronze limbs, and thought resignedly that a seventeen-year-old girl could find the strangest sorts of love objects. But he was happy to see that they were all evidently pleased with the robot. Even with the discount and the trade-in, it *had* been a little on the costly side.

But it would be worth it.

Carmichael slept soundly and woke early, anticipating

the first breakfast under the new regime. He still felt pleased with himself.

Dieting had always been such a nuisance, he thought—but, on the other hand, he had never enjoyed the sensation of an annoying roll of fat pushing outward against his elastobelt. He exercised sporadically, but it did little good, and he never had the initiative to keep a rigorous dieting campaign going for long. Now, though, with the mathematics of reducing done effortlessly for him, all the calculating and cooking being handled by the new robot—now, for the first time since he had been Joey's age, he could look forward to being slim and trim once again.

He dressed, showered and hastily depilated. It was 0730. Breakfast was ready.

Ethel and the children were already at the table when he arrived. Ethel and Myra were munching toast; Joey was peering at a bowl of milkless dry cereal, next to which stood a full glass of milk. Carmichael sat down.

"Your toast, sir," the roboservitor murmured.

Carmichael stared at the single slice. It had already been buttered for him, and the butter had evidently been measured out with a micrometer. The robot proceeded to hand him a cup of black coffee.

He groped for the cream and sugar. They weren't anywhere on the table. The other members of his family were regarding him strangely, and they were curiously, suspiciously silent.

"I like cream and sugar in my coffee," he said to the hovering roboservitor. "Didn't you find that in Jemima's old recipe bank?"

"Of course, sir. But you must learn to drink your coffee without such things, if you wish to lose weight."

Carmichael chuckled. Somehow he had not expected the regimen to be quite like this—quite so, well, Spartan. "Oh, yes. Of course. Ah—are the eggs ready yet?" He considered a day incomplete unless he began it with soft-boiled eggs.

"Sorry, no sir. On Mondays, Wednesdays and Fridays, breakfast is to consist of toast and black coffee only, except for Master Joey, who gets cereal, fruit juice and milk."

"I—see."

Well, he had asked for it. He shrugged and took a bite of the toast. He sipped the coffee; it tasted like river mud, but he tried not to make a face.

Joey seemed to be going about the business of eating his cereal rather oddly, Carmichael noticed next. "Why don't you pour that glass of milk *into* the cereal?" he asked. "Won't it taste better that way?"

"Sure it will. But Bismarck says I won't get another glass if I do, so I'm eating it this way."

"Bismarck?"

Joey grinned. "It's the name of a famous 19th-Century German dictator. They called him the Iron Chancellor." He jerked his head toward the kitchen, to which the roboservitor had silently retreated. "Pretty good name for him, eh?"

"No," said Carmichael. "It's silly."

"It has a certain ring of truth, though," Ethel remarked.

Carmichael did not reply. He finished his toast and coffee somewhat glumly and signalled Clyde to get the car out of the garage. He felt depressed—dieting didn't seem to be so effortless after all, even with the new robot.

As he walked toward the door, the robot glided around him and handed him a small printed slip of paper. Carmichael stared at it. It said:

FRUIT JUICE
LETTUCE & TOMATO SALAD
(ONE) HARD-BOILED EGG
BLACK COFFEE

"What is this thing?"

"You are the only member of this family group who will not be eating three meals a day under my personal supervision. This is your luncheon menu. Please adhere to it," the robot said smoothly.

Repressing a sputter, Carmichael said, "Yes—yes. Of course."

He pocketed the menu and made his way uncertainly to the waiting car.

He was faithful to the robot's orders at lunchtime that day; even though he was beginning to develop resistance to the idea that had seemed so appealing only the night before, he was willing, at least, to give it a try.

But something prompted him to stay away from the restaurant where Normandy Trust employees usually lunched, and where there were human waiters to smirk at him and fellow executives to ask prying questions.

He ate instead at a cheap robocafeteria two blocks to the north. He slipped in surreptitiously with his collar turned up, punched out his order (it cost him less than a credit altogether) and wolfed it down. He still felt hungry when he had finished, but he compelled himself to return loyally to the office.

He wondered how long he was going to be able to keep up this iron self-control. Not very long, he realized dolefully. And if anyone from the company caught him eating at a robocafeteria, he'd be a laughing stock. Some-one of executive status just *didn't* eat lunch by himself in mechanized cafeterias.

By the time he had finished his day's work, his stomach felt knotted and pleated. His hand was shaky as he punched out his destination on the car's autopanel, and he was thankful that it took less than an hour to get home from the office. Soon, he thought, he'd be tasting food again. Soon. Soon. He switched on the roof-mounted video, leaned back at the recliner and tried to relax as the car bore him homeward.

He was in for a surprise, though, when he stepped through the safety field into his home. Clyde was waiting as always, and, as always, took his hat and cloak. And, as always, Carmichael reached out for the cocktail that Clyde prepared nightly to welcome him home.

There was no cocktail.

"Are we out of gin, Clyde?"

"No, sir."

"How come no drink, then?"

The robot's rubberized metallic features seemed to drop. "Because, sir, a Martini's caloric content is inordinately high. Gin is rated at a hundred calories per ounce and—"

"Oh, no. You too!"

"Pardon, sir. The new roboservitor has altered my responsive circuits to comply with the regulations now in force in this household."

Carmichael felt his fingers starting to tremble. "Clyde, you've been my butler for almost twenty years."

"Yes, sir."

"You always make my drinks for me. You mix the best Martinis in the Western Hemisphere."

"Thank you, sir."

"And you're going to mix one for me right now! That's a direct order!"

"Sir! I—" The robutler staggered wildly and nearly careened into Carmichael. It seemed to have lost all control over its gyro-balance; it clutched agonizedly at its chest panel and started to sag.

Hastily, Carmichael barked, "Order countermanded! Clyde, are you all right?"

Slowly, and with a creak, the robot straightened up. It looked dangerously close to an overload. "Your direct order set up a first-level conflict in me, sir," Clyde whispered faintly. "I—came close to burning out just then, sir. May—may I be excused?"

"Of course. Sorry, Clyde." Carmichael balled his fists.

There was such a thing as going too far! The robo-servitor—Bismarck—had obviously placed on Clyde a flat prohibition against serving liquor to him. Reducing or no reducing, there were *limits*.

Carmichael strode angrily toward the kitchen.

His wife met him halfway. "I didn't hear you come in, Sam. I want to talk to you about—"

"Later. Where's that robot?"

"In the kitchen, I imagine. It's almost dinnertime."

He brushed past her and swept on into the kitchen, where Bismarck was moving efficiently from electro-stove to magnetic worktable. The robot swivelled as Carmichael entered.

"Did you have a good day, sir?"

"No! I'm hungry!"

"The first days of a diet are always the most difficult Mr. Carmichael. But your body will ajdust to the reduction in food intake before long."

"I'm sure of that. But what's this business of tinkering with Clyde?"

"The butler insisted on preparing an alcoholic drink for you. I was forced to adjust his programming. From now on, sir, you may indulge in cocktails on Tuesdays, Thursdays, and Saturdays. I beg to be excused from further discussion now, sir. The meal is almost ready."

Poor Clyde! Carmichael thought. *And poor me!* He gnashed his teeth impotently a few times, then gave up and turned away from the glistening, overbearing roboservitor. A light gleamed on the side of the robot's head, indicating that he had shut off his audio circuits and was totally engaged in his task.

Dinner consisted of steak and peas, followed by black coffee. The steak was rare; Carmichael preferred it well done. But Bismarck—the name was beginning to take hold—had had all the latest dietetic theories taped into him, and rare meat it was.

After the robot had cleared the table and tidied up the kitchen, it retired to its storage place in the basement, which gave the Carmichael family a chance to speak openly to each other for the first time that evening.

"Lord!" Ethel snorted. "Sam, I don't object to losing weight, but if we're going to be *tyrannized* in our own home—"

"Mom's right," Joey put in. "It doesn't seem fair for that thing to feed us whatever it pleases. And I didn't like the way it messed around with Clyde's circuits."

Carmichael spread his hands. "I'm not happy about it either. But we have to give it a try. We can always make readjustments in the programming if it turns out to be necessary."

"But how long are we going to keep this up?" Myra wanted to know. "I had three meals in this house today and I'm starved!"

"Me, too," Joey said. He elbowed himself from his chair and looked around. "Bismarck's downstairs. I'm going to get a slice of lemon pie while the coast is clear."

"No!" Carmichael thundered.

"No?"

"There's no sense in my spending three thousand credits on a dietary robot if you're going to cheat, Joey. I forbid you to have any pie."

"But, Dad, I'm hungry! I'm a growing boy! I'm—"

"You're sixteen years old, and if you grow much more, you won't fit inside the house," Carmichael snapped, looking up at his six-foot-one son.

"Sam, we can't starve the boy," Ethel protested. "If he wants pie, let him have some. You're carrying this reduction fetish too far."

Carmichael considered that. Perhaps, he thought, I *am* being a little over severe. And the thought of lemon pie was a tempting one. He was pretty hungry himself.

"All right," he said with feigned reluctance. "I guess a bit of pie won't wreck the plan. In fact, I suppose I'll have some myself. Joey, why don't you—"

"Begging your pardon," a purring voice said behind him. Carmichael jumped half an inch. It was the robot, Bismarck. "It would be most unfortunate if you were to have pie now, Mr. Carmichael. My calculations are very precise."

Carmichael saw the angry gleam in his son's eye, but the robot seemed extraordinarily big at that moment, and it happened to stand between him and the kitchen.

He sighed weakly. "Let's forget the lemon pie, Joey."

After two full days of the Bismarckian diet, Carmichael discovered that his inner resources of will power were beginning to crumble. On the third day he tossed away the printed lunchtime diet and went out irresponsibly with MacDougal and Hennessey for a six-course lunch, complete with cocktails. It seemed to him that he hadn't tasted real food since the robot arrived.

That night, he was able to tolerate the seven-hundred-calorie dinner without any inward grumblings, being still well lined with lunch. But Ethel and Myra and Joey were increasingly irritable. It seemed that the robot had usurped Ethel's job of handling the daily marketing and had stocked in nothing but a huge supply of healthy low-calorie foods. The larder now bulged with wheat germ, protein bread, irrigated salmon, and other hitherto unfamiliar items. Myra had taken up biting her nails; Joey's mood was one of black sullen brooding, and Carmichael knew how that could lead to trouble quickly with a sixteen-year-old.

After the meager dinner, he ordered Bismarck to go to the basement and stay there until summoned.

The robot said, "I must advise you, sir, that I will detect indulgence in any forbidden foods in my absence and adjust for it in the next meals."

"You have my word," Carmichael said, thinking it was indeed queer to have to pledge on your honor to your own robot. He waited until the massive servitor had vanished below; then he turned to Joey and said, "Get the instruction manual, boy."

Joey grinned in understanding. Ethel said, "Sam, what are you going to do?"

Carmichael patted his shrunken waistline. "I'm going to take a can opener to that creature and adjust his programming. He's overdoing this diet business. Joey, have you found the instructions on how to reprogram the robot?"

"Page 167. I'll get the tool kit, Dad."

"Right." Carmichael turned to the robutler, who was standing by dumbly, in his usual forward-stooping posture of expectancy. "Clyde, go down below and tell Bismarck we want him right away."

Moments later, the two robots appeared. Carmichael said to the roboservitor, "I'm afraid it's necessary for us to change your program. We've overestimated our capacity for losing weight."

"I beg you to reconsider, sir. Extra weight is harmful to every vital organ in the body. I plead with you to maintain my scheduling unaltered."

"I'd rather cut my own throat. Joey, inactivate him and do your stuff."

Grinning fiercely, the boy stepped forward and pressed the stud that opened the robot's ribcage. A frightening assortment of gears, cams and translucent cables became visible inside the robot. With a small wrench in one hand and the open instruction book in the other, Joey prepared to make the necessary changes, while Carmichael held his breath and a pall of silence descended on the living room. Even old Clyde leaned forward to have a better view.

Joey muttered, "Lever F2, with the yellow indicia, is to be advanced one notch . . . umm. Now twist Dial B9 to the left, thereby opening the taping compartment and—oops!"

Carmichael heard the clang of a wrench and saw the bright flare of sparks; Joey leaped back, cursing with surprisingly mature skill. Ethel and Myra gasped simultaneously.

"What happened?" four voices—Clyde's coming in last demanded.

"Dropped the damn wrench," Joey said. "I guess I shorted out something in there."

The robot's eyes were whirling satanically and its voice box was emitting an awesome twelve-cycle rumble. The great metal creature stood stiffly in the middle of the living room; with brusque gestures of its big hands, it slammed shut the open chest plates.

"We'd better call Mr. Robinson," Ethel said worriedly. "A short-circuited robot is likely to explode, or worse."

"We should have called Robinson in the first place," Carmichael murmured bitterly. "It's my fault for letting Joey tinker with an expensive and delicate mechanism like that. Myra, get me the card Mr. Robinson left."

"Gee, Dad, this is the first time I've ever had anything like that go wrong," Joey insisted. "I didn't know—"

"You're darned right you didn't know." Carmichael took the card from his daughter and started toward the phone. "I hope we can reach him at this hour. If we can't—"

Suddenly Carmichael felt cold fingers prying the card from his hand. He was so startled he relinquished it without a struggle. He watched as Bismarck efficiently ripped it into little fragments and shoved them into a wall disposal unit.

The robot said, "There will be no further meddling with my program tapes." Its voice was deep and strangely harsh.

"What—"

"Mr. Carmichael, today you violated the program I set down for you. My perceptors reveal that you consumed an amount far in excess of your daily lunchtime requirement."

"Sam, what—"

"Quiet, Ethel. Bismarck, I order you to shut yourself off at once."

"My apologies, sir. I cannot serve you if I am shut off."

"I don't *want* you to serve me. You're out of order. I want you to remain still until I can phone the repairman and get him to service you."

Then he remembered the card that had gone into the disposal unit. He felt a faint tremor of apprehension.

"You took Robinson's card and destroyed it."

"Further alteration of my circuits would be detrimental to the Carmichael family," said the robot. "I cannot permit you to summon the repairman."

"Don't get him angry, Dad," Joey warned. "I'll call the police. I'll be back in—"

"You will remain within this house," the robot said. Moving with impressive speed on its oiled treads, it crossed the room, blocking the door, and reached far above its head to activate the impassable privacy field that protected the house. Carmichael watched, aghast, as the inexorable robotic fingers twisted and manipulated the field controls.

"I have now reversed the polarity of the house privacy field," the robot announced. "Since you are obviously not to be trusted to keep to the diet I prescribe, I cannot allow you to leave the premises. You will remain within and continue to obey my beneficial advice."

Calmly, he uprooted the telephone. Next, the windows were opaqued and the stud broken off. Finally, the robot seized the instruction book from Joey's numbed hands and shoved it into the disposal unit.

"Breakfast will be served at the usual time," Bismarck said mildly. "For optimum purposes of health, you are all to be asleep by 2300 hours. I shall leave you now, until morning. Good night."

Carmichael did not sleep well that night, nor did he eat well the next day. He awoke late, for one thing—

well past nine. He discovered that someone, obviously Bismarck, had neatly cancelled out the impulses from the housebrain that woke him at seven each morning.

The breakfast menu was toast and black coffee. Carmichael ate disgruntedly, not speaking, indicating by brusque scowls that he did not want to be spoken to. After the miserable meal had been cleared away, he surreptitiously tiptoed to the front door in his dressing gown and darted a hand toward the handle.

The door refused to budge. He pushed until sweat dribbled down his face. He heard Ethel whisper warningly, *"Sam—"* and a moment later cool metallic fingers gently disengaged him from the door.

Bismarck said, "I beg your pardon, sir. The door will not open. I explained this last night."

Carmichael gazed sourly at the gimmicked control box of the privacy field. The robot had them utterly hemmed in. The reversed privacy field made it impossible for them to leave the house; it cast a sphere of force around the entire detached dwelling. In theory, the field could be penetrated from outside, but nobody was likely to come calling without an invitation. Not here in Westley. It wasn't one of those neighborly subdivisions where everybody knew everybody else. Carmichael had picked it for that reason.

"Damn you," he growled, "you can't hold us *prisoners* in here!"

"My intent is only to help you," said the robot, in a mechanical yet dedicated voice. "My function is to supervise your diet. Since you will not obey willingly, obedience must be enforced—for your own good."

Carmichael scowled and walked away. The worst part of it was that the roboservitor sounded so *sincere!*

Trapped. The phone connection was severed. The windows were darkened. Somehow, Joey's attempt at repairs had resulted in a short circuit of the robot's obedience filters, and had also exaggeratedly stimulated its sense of function. Now Bismarck was determined to make them lose weight if it had to kill them to do so.

And that seemed very likely.

Blockaded, the Carmichael family met in a huddled little group to whisper plans for a counterattack. Clyde stood watch, but the robutler seemed to be in a state of general shock since the demonstration of the servitor-robot's independent capacity for action, and Carmichael now regarded him as undependable.

"He's got the kitchen walled off with some kind of electronic-based force web," Joey said. "He must have built it during the night. I tried to sneak in and scrounge some food, and got nothing but a flat nose for trying."

"I know," Carmichael said sadly. "He built the same sort of doohickey around the bar. Three hundred credits of good booze in there and I can't even grab the handle!"

"This is no time to worry about drinking," Ethel said morosely. "We'll be skeletons any day."

"It isn't *that* bad, Mom!" Joey said.

"Yes, it is!" cried Myra. "I've lost five pounds in four days!"

"Is that so terrible?"

"I'm wasting away," she sobbed. "My figure—it's vanishing! And—"

"Quiet," Carmichael whispered. "Bismarck's coming!"

The robot emerged from the kitchen, passing through the force barrier as if it had been a cobweb. It seemed to have effect on humans only, Carmichael thought. "Lunch will be served in eight minutes," it said obsequiously, and returned to its lair.

Carmichael glanced at his watch. The time was 1230 hours. "Probably down at the office they're wondering where I am," he said. "I haven't missed a day's work in years."

"They won't care," Ethel said. "An executive isn't required to account for every day off he takes, you know.

"But they'll worry after three or four days, won't they?" Myra asked. "Maybe they'll try to phone—or even send a rescue mission!"

From the kitchen, Bismarck said coldly, "There will be no danger of that. While you slept this morning, I notified your place of employment that you were resigning."

Carmichael gasped. Then, recovering, he said: "You're lying! The phone's cut off—and you never would have risked leaving the house, even if we *were* asleep!"

"I communicated with them via a microwave generator I constructed with the aid of your son's reference books last night," Bismarck replied. "Clyde reluctantly supplied me with the number. I also phoned your bank and instructed them to handle for you all such matters as tax payments, investment decisions, etc. To forestall difficulties, let me add that a force web will prevent access on your part to the electronic equipment in the basement. I will be able to conduct such communication with the outside world as will be necessary for your welfare, Mr. Carmichael. You need have no worries on that score."

"No," Carmichael echoed hollowly. "No worries."

He turned to Joey. "We've got to get out of here. Are you sure there's no way of disconnecting the privacy field?"

"He's got one of his force fields rigged around the control box. I can't even get near the thing."

"If only we had an iceman, or an oilman, the way the oldtime houses did," Ethel said bitterly. "He'd show up and come inside and probably he'd know how to shut the field off. But not *here*. Oh no. We've got a shiny chrome-plated cryostat in the basement that dishes out lots of liquid helium to run the fancy cryotronic super-cooled power plant that gives us heat and light, and we have enough food in the freezer to last for at least a decade or two, and so we can live like this for years, a neat little self-contained island in the middle of civilization, with nobody bothering us, nobody wondering about us, and Sam Carmichael's pet robot to feed us whenever and as little as it pleases—"

There was a cutting edge to her voice that was dangerously close to hysteria.

"Ethel, please," said Carmichael.

"Please what? Please keep quiet? Please stay calm? Sam, we're *prisoners* in here!"

"I know. You don't have to raise your voice."

"Maybe if I do, someone will hear us and come and get us out," she replied more coolly.

"It's four hundred feet to the next home, dear. And in the seven years we've lived here, we've had about two visits from our neighbors. We paid a stiff price for seclusion and now we're paying a stiffer one. But please keep under control, Ethel."

"Don't worry, Mom. I'll figure a way out of this," Joey said reassuringly.

In one corner of the living room, Myra was sobbing quietly to herself, blotching her makeup. Carmichael felt a faintly claustrophobic quiver. The house was big, three levels and twelve rooms, but even so he could get tired of it very quickly.

"Luncheon is served," the roboservitor announced in booming tones.

And tired of lettuce-and-tomato lunches, too, Carmichael added silently, as he shepherded his family toward the dining room for their meagre midday meal.

"You have to do *something* about this, Sam," Ethel Carmichael said on the third day of their imprisonment.

He glared at her. "Have to, eh? And just what am I supposed to do?"

"Daddy, don't get excited," Myra said.

He whirled on her. "Don't tell me what I should or shouldn't do!"

"She can't help it, dear. We're all a little overwrought. After all, cooped up here—"

"I know. Like lambs in a pen," he finished acidly. "Except that we're not being fattened for slaughter. We're—we're being *thinned,* and for our own alleged good!"

Carmichael subsided gloomily. Toast-and-black-coffee, lettuce-and-tomato, rare-steak-and-peas. Bismarck's channels seemed to have frozen permanently at that daily menu.

But what could he do?

Contact with the outside world was impossible. The robot had erected a bastion in the basement from which he conducted such little business with the world as the Carmichael family had. Generally, they were self-sufficient. And Bismarck's force fields insured the impossibility of any attempts to disconnect the outer sheath, break into the basement, or even get at the food supply or the liquor. It was all very neat, and the four of them were fast approaching a state of starvation.

"Sam?"

He lifted his head wearily. "What is it, Ethel?"

"Myra had an idea before. Tell him, Myra."

"Oh, it would never work," Myra said demurely.

"Tell *him!*"

"Well—Dad, you *could* try to turn Bismarck off."

"Huh?" Carmichael grunted.

"I mean if you or Joey could distract him somehow, then Joey or you could open him up again and—"

"No," Carmichael snapped. "That thing's seven feet tall and weighs three hundred pounds. If you think *I'm* going to wrestle with it—"

"We could let Clyde try," Ethel suggested.

Carmichael shook his head vehemently. "The carnage would be frightful."

Joey said, "Dad, it may be our only hope."

"You too?" Carmichael asked.

He took a deep breath. He felt himself speared by two deadly feminine glances, and he knew there was no hope but to try it. Resignedly, he pushed himself to his feet and said, "Okay. Clyde, go call Bismarck. Joey, I'll try to hang onto his arms while you open up his chest. Yank anything you can."

"Be careful," Ethel warned. "If there's an explosion—"

"If there's an explosion, we're all free," Carmichael said testily. He turned to see the broad figure of the roboservitor standing at the entrance to the living room.

"May I be of service, sir?"

"You may," Carmichael said. "We're having a little debate here and we want your evidence. It's a matter of defannising the poozlestan and—*Joey, open him up!*"

Carmichael grabbed for the robot's arms, trying to hold them without getting hurled across the room, while his son clawed frantically at the stud that opened the robot's innards. Carmichael anticipated immediate destruction—but, to his surprise, he found himself slipping as he tried to grasp the thick arms.

"Dad, it's no use. I—he—"

Carmichael found himself abruptly four feet off the ground. He heard Ethel and Myra scream and Clyde's, *"Do* be careful, sir."

Bismarck was carrying them across the room, gently, cradling him in one giant arm and Joey in the other. It set them down on the couch and stood back.

"Such an attempt is highly dangerous," Bismarck said reprovingly. "It puts me in danger of harming you physically. Please avoid any such acts in the future."

Carmichael stared broodingly at his son. "Did you have the same trouble I did?"

Joey nodded. "I couldn't get within an inch of his skin. It stands to reason, though. He's built one of those damned force screens around *himself,* too!"

Carmichael groaned. He did not look at his wife and his children. Physical attack on Bismarck was now out of the question. He began to feel as if he had been condemned to life imprisonment—and that his stay in durance vile would not be extremely prolonged.

In the upstairs bathroom, six days after the beginning of the blockade, Sam Carmichael stared at his haggard fleshless face in the mirror before wearily climbing on the scale.

He weighed 180.

He had lost twelve pounds in less than two weeks. He was fast becoming a quivering wreck.

A thought occurred to him as he stared at the wavering needle on the scale, and sudden elation spread over him. He dashed downstairs. Ethel was doggedly crocheting in the living room; Joey and Myra were playing cards grimly, desperately now, after six solid days of gin rummy and honeymoon bridge.

"Where's that robot?" Carmichael roared. "Come out here!"

"In the kitchen," Ethel said tonelessly.

"Bismarck! Bismarck!" Carmichael roared. "Come out here!"

The robot appeared. "How may I serve you sir?"

"Damn you, scan me with your superpower receptors and tell me how much I weigh!"

After a pause, the robot said gravely, "One hundred seventy-nine pounds eleven ounces, Mr. Carmichael."

"Yes! Yes! And the original program I had taped into you was supposed to reduce me from 192 to 180," Carmichael crowed triumphantly. "So I'm finished with you, as long as I don't gain any more weight. And so are the rest of us, I'll bet. Ethel! Myra! Joey! Upstairs and weigh yourselves!"

But the robot regarded him with a doleful glare and said, "Sir, I find no record within me of any limitation on your reduction of weight."

"What?"

"I have checked my tapes fully. I have a record of an order causing weight reduction, but that tape does not appear to specify a *terminus ad quem*."

Carmichael exhaled and took three staggering steps backward. His legs wobbled; he felt Joey supporting him. He mumbled, "But I thought—I'm sure we did—I *know* we instructed you—"

Hunger gnawed at his flesh. Joey said softly, "Dad, probably that part of his tape was erased when he short-circuited."

"Oh," Carmichael said numbly.

He tottered into the living room and collapsed heavily in what had once been his favorite armchair. It wasn't anymore. The entire house had become odious to him. He longed to see the sunlight again, to see trees and grass, even to see that excrescence of an ultramodern house that the left-hand neighbors had erected.

But now that would be impossible. He had hoped, for a few minutes at least, that the robot would release them from dietary bondage when the original goal was shown to be accomplished. Evidently that was to be denied him. He giggled, then began to laugh.

"What's so funny, dear?" Ethel asked. She had lost her earlier tendencies to hysteria, and after long days of complex crocheting now regarded the universe with quiet resignation.

"Funny? The fact that I weight 180 now. I'm lean, trim, fit as a fiddle. Next month I'll weigh 170. Then 160. Then finally about 88 pounds or so. We'll all shrivel up. Bismarck will starve us to death."

"Don't worry, Dad. We're going to get out of this."

Somehow Joey's brash boyish confidence sounded forced now. Carmichael shook his head. "We won't. We'll never get out. And Bismarck's going to reduce us *ad infinitum*. He's got no *terminus ad quem!*"

"What's he saying?" Myra asked.

"It's Latin," Joey explained. "But listen, Dad—I have an idea that I think will work." He lowered his voice. "I'm going to try to adjust Clyde, see? If I can get a sort of multiple vibrating effect in his neural pathway, maybe I can slip him through the reversed privacy field. He can go get help, find someone who can shut the field off. There's an article on multiphase generators in last month's *Popular Electromagnetics* and it's in my room upstairs. I—"

His voice died away. Carmichael, who had been listening with the air of a condemned man hearing his reprieve, said impatiently, "Well? Go on. Tell me more."

"Didn't you hear that, Dad?"

"Hear what?"

"The front door. I thought I heard it open just now."

"We're all cracking up," Carmichael said dully. He cursed the salesman at Marhew, he cursed the inventor of cryotronic robots, he cursed the day he had first felt ashamed of good old Jemima and resolved to replace her with a new model.

"I hope I'm not intruding, Mr. Carmichael," a new voice said apologetically.

Carmichael blinked and looked up. A wiry, ruddy-cheeked figure in a heavy peajacket had materialized in the middle of the living room. He was clutching a green metal toolbox in one gloved hand. He was Robinson, the robot repairman.

Carmichael asked hoarsely, "How did *you* get in?"

"Through the front door. I could see a light on inside, but nobody answered the doorbell when I rang, so I stepped in. Your doorbell's out of order. I thought I'd tell you. I know it's rude—"

"Don't apologize," Carmichael muttered. "We're delighted to see you."

"I was in the neighborhood, you see, and I figured

I'd drop in and see how things were working out with your new robot," Robinson said.

Carmichael told him crisply and precisely and quickly. "So we've been prisoners in here for six days," he finished. "And your robot is gradually starving us to death. We can't hold out much longer."

The smile abruptly left Robinson's cheery face. "I *thought* you all looked rather unhealthy. Oh, damn, now there'll be an investigation and all kinds of trouble. But at least I can end your imprisonment."

He opened his toolbox and selected a tubular instrument eight inches long, with a glass bulb at one end and a trigger attachment at the other. "Force-field damper," he explained. He pointed it at the control box of the privacy field and nodded in satisfaction. "There. Great little gadget. That neutralizes the effects of what the robot did and you're no longer blockaded. And now, if you'll produce the robot—"

Carmichael sent Clyde off to get Bismarck. The robutler returned a few moments later, followed by the looming roboservitor. Robinson grinned gaily, pointed the neutralizer at Bismarck and squeezed. The robot froze in mid-glide, emitting a brief squeak.

"There. That should immobilize him. Let's have a look in that chassis now."

The repairman quickly opened Bismarck's chest and, producing a pocket flash, peered around in the complex interior of the servomechanism, making occasional clucking inaudible comments.

Overwhelmed with relief, Carmichael shakily made his way to a seat. Free! Free at last! His mouth watered at the thought of the meals he was going to have in the next few days. Potatoes and Martinis and warm buttered rolls and all the other forbidden foods!

"Fascinating," Robinson said, half to himself. "The obedience filters are completely shorted out, and the purpose nodes were somehow soldered together by the momentary high-voltage arc. I've never seen anything quite like this, you know."

"Neither had we," Carmichael said hollowly.

"Really, though—this is an utterly new breakthrough in robotic science! If we can reproduce this effect, it means we can build self-willed robots—and think of what *that* means to science!"

"We know already," Ethel said.

"I'd love to watch what happens when the power source is operating," Robinson went on. "For instance, is that feedback loop really negative or—"

"No!" five voices shrieked at once—with Clyde, as usual, coming in last.

It was too late. The entire event had taken no more than a tenth of a second. Robinson had squeezed his neutralizer trigger again, activating Bismarck—and in one quick swoop the roboservitor seized neutralizer and toolbox from the stunned repairman, activated the privacy field once again, and exultantly crushed the fragile neutralizer between two mighty fingers.

Robinson stammered, "but—but—"

"This attempt at interfering with the well-being of the Carmichael family was ill-advised," Bismarck said severely. He peered into the toolbox, found a second neutralizer and neatly reduced it to junk. He clanged shut his chest plates.

Robinson turned and streaked for the door, forgetting the reactivated privacy field. He bounced back hard, spinning wildly around. Carmichael rose from his seat just in time to catch him.

There was a panicky, trapped look on the repairman's face. Carmichael was no longer able to share the emotion; inwardly he was numb, totally resigned, not minded for further struggle.

"He—he moved so *fast!*" Robinson burst out.

"He did indeed," Carmichael said tranquilly. He patted his hollow stomach and sighed gently. "Luckily, we have an unoccupied guest bedroom for you, Mr. Robinson. Welcome to our happy little home. I hope you like toast and black coffee for breakfast."

THE REALITY TRIP

I am a reclamation project for her. She lives on my floor of the hotel, a dozen rooms down the hall: a lady poet, private income. No, that makes her sound too old, a middle-aged eccentric. Actually she is no more than thirty. Taller than I am, with long kinky brown hair and a sharp, bony nose that has a bump on the bridge. Eyes are very glossy. A studied raggedness about her dress; carefully chosen shabby clothes. I am in no position really to judge the sexual attractiveness of Earthfolk but I gather from remarks made by men living here that she is not considered good-looking. I pass her often on my way to my room. She smiles fiercely at me. Saying to herself, no doubt, You poor lonely man. Let me help you bear the burden of your unhappy life. Let me show you the meaning of love, for I too know what it is like to be alone.

Or words to that effect. She's never actually said any such thing. But her intentions are transparent. When she sees me, a kind of hunger comes into her eyes, part maternal, part (I guess) sexual, and her face takes on a wild crazy intensity. Burning with emotion. Her name is

29

Elizabeth Cooke. "Are you fond of poetry, Mr. Knecht?" she asked me this morning, as we creaked upward together in the ancient elevator. And an hour later she knocked at my door. "Something for you to read," she said. "I wrote them." A sheaf of large yellow sheets, stapled at the top; poems printed in smeary blue mimeography. *The Reality Trip,* the collection was headed. *Limited Edition: 125 Copies.* "You can keep it if you like," she explained. "I've got lots more." She was wearing bright corduroy slacks and a flimsy pink shawl through which her breasts plainly showed. Small tapering breasts, not very functional-looking. When she saw me studying them her nostrils flared momentarily and she blinked her eyes three times swiftly. Tokens of lust?

I read the poems. Is it fair for me to offer judgment on them? Even though I've lived on this planet eleven of its years, even though my command of colloquial English is quite good, do I really comprehend the inner life of poetry? I thought they were all quite bad. Earnest, plodding poems, capturing what they call slices of life. The world around her, the cruel, brutal, unloving city. Lamenting the failure of the people to open to one another. The title poem began this way:

> *He was on the reality trip. Big black man,*
> *bloodshot eyes, bad teeth. Eisenhower jacket,*
> *frayed. Smell of cheap wine. I guess a knife in*
> *his pocket. Looked at me mean. Criminal*
> *record. Rape, child-beating, possession of drugs.*
> *In his head saying, slavemistress bitch, and me*
> *in my head saying, black brother, let's freak in*
> *together, let's trip on love—*

And so forth. Warm, direct emotion; but is the urge to love all wounded things a sufficient center for poetry? I don't know. I did put her poems through the scanner and transmit them to Homeworld, although I doubt they'll learn much from them about Earth. It would flatter Elizabeth to know that while she has few readers here, she has acquired some ninety light-years away. But of course I can't tell her that.

She came back a short while ago. "Did you like them?" she asked.

"Very much. You have such sympathy for those who suffer."

I think she expected me to invite her in. I was careful not to look at her breasts this time.

The hotel is on West 23rd Street. It must be over a hundred years old; the façade is practically baroque and the interior shows a kind of genteel decay. The place has a bohemian tradition. Most of its guests are permanent residents and many of them are artists, novelists, playwrights, and such. I have lived here nine years. I know a number of the residents by name, and they me, but I have discouraged any real intimacy, naturally, and everyone has respected that choice. I do not invite others into my room. Sometimes I let myself be invited to visit theirs, since one of my responsibilities on this world is to get to know something of the way Earthfolk live and think. Elizabeth is the first to attempt to cross the invisible barrier of privacy I surround myself with. I'm not sure how I'll handle that. She moved in about three years ago; her attentions became noticeable perhaps ten months back, and for the last five or six weeks she's been a great nuisance. Some kind of confrontation is inevitable: either I must tell her to leave me alone, or I will find myself drawn into a situation impossible to tolerate. Perhaps she'll find someone else to feel even sorrier for, before it comes to that.

My daily routine rarely varies. I rise at seven. First Feeding. Then I clean my skin (my outer one, the Earth-skin, I mean) and dress. From eight to ten I transmit data to Homeworld. Then I go out for the morning field trip:

talking to people, buying newspapers, often some library research. At one I return to my room. Second Feeding. I transmit data from two to five. Out again, perhaps to the theater, to a motion picture, to a political meeting. I must soak up the flavor of this planet. Often to saloons; I am equipped for ingesting alcohol, though of course I must get rid of it before it has been in my body very long, and I drink and listen and sometimes argue. At midnight back to my room. Third Feeding. Transmit data from one to four in the morning. Then three hours of sleep, and at seven the cycle begins anew. It is a comforting schedule. I don't know how many agents Homeworld has on Earth, but I like to think that I'm one of the most diligent and useful. I miss very little. I've done good service, and, as they say here, hard work is its own reward. I won't deny that I hate the physical discomfort of it and frequently give way to real despair over my isolation from my own kind. Sometimes I even think of asking for a transfer to Homeworld. But what would become of me there? What services could I perform? I have shaped my life to one end: that of dwelling among the Earthfolk and reporting on their ways. If I give that up, I am nothing.

Of course there is the physical pain. Which is considerable.

The gravitational pull of Earth is almost twice that of Homeworld. It makes for a leaden life for me. My inner organs always sagging against the lower rim of my carapace. My muscles cracking with strain. Every movement a willed effort. My heart in constant protest. In my eleven years I have as one might expect adapted somewhat to the conditions; I have toughened, I have thickened. I suspect that if I were transported instantly to Homeworld now I would be quite giddy, baffled by the lightness of everything. I would leap and soar and stumble, and might even miss this crushing pull of Earth. Yet

I doubt that. I suffer here; at all times the weight oppresses me. Not to sound too self-pitying about it, I knew the conditions in advance. I was placed in simulated Earth gravity when I volunteered, and was given a chance to withdraw, and I decided to go anyway. Not realizing that a week under double gravity is not the same thing as a lifetime. I could always have stepped out of the simulation chamber. Not here. The eternal drag on every molecule of me. The pressure. My flesh is always in mourning.

And the outer body I must wear. This cunning disguise. Forever to be swaddled in thick masses of synthetic flesh, smothering me, engulfing me. The soft slippery slap of it against the self within. The elaborate framework that holds it erect, by which I make it move: a forest of struts and braces and servoactuators and cables, in the midst of which I must unendingly huddle, atop my little platform in the gut. Adopting one or another of various uncomfortable positions, constantly shifting and squirming, now jabbing myself on some awkwardly placed projection, now trying to make my inflexible body flexibly to bend. Seeing the world by periscope through mechanical eyes. Enwombed in this mountain of meat. It is a clever thing; it must look convincingly human, since no one has ever doubted me, and it ages ever so slightly from year to year, greying a bit at the temples, thickening a bit at the paunch. It walks. It talks. It takes in food and drink, when it has to. (And deposits them in a removable pouch near my leftmost arm.) And I within it. The hidden chess player; the invisible rider. If I dared, I would periodically strip myself of this cloak of flesh and crawl around my room in my own guise. But it is forbidden. Eleven years now and I have not been outside my protoplasmic housing. I feel sometimes that it has come to adhere to me, that it is no longer merely around me but by now a part of me.

In order to eat I must unseal it at the middle, a process

that takes many minutes. Three times a day I unbutton myself so that I can stuff the food concentrates into my true gullet. Faulty design, I call that. They could just as easily have arranged it so I could pop the food into my Earthmouth and have it land in my own digestive tract. I suppose the newer models have that. Excretion is just as troublesome for me; I unseal, reach in, remove the cubes of waste, seal my skin again. Down the toilet with them. A nuisance.

And the loneliness! To look at the stars and know Homeworld is out there somewhere! To think of all the others, mating, chanting, dividing, abstracting, while I live out my days in this crumbling hotel on an alien planet, tugged down by gravity and locked within a cramped counterfeit body—always alone, always pretending that I am not what I am and that I am what I am not, spying, questioning, recording, reporting, coping with the misery of solitude, hunting for the comforts of philosophy—

In all of this there is only one real consolation, aside, that is, from the pleasure of knowing that I am of service to Homeworld. The atmosphere of New York City grows grimier every year. The streets are full of crude vehicles belching undigested hydrocarbons. To the Earthfolk, this stuff is pollution, and they mutter worriedly about it. To me it is joy. It is the only touch of Homeworld here: that sweet soup of organic compounds adrift in the air. It intoxicates me. I walk down the street breathing deeply, sucking the good molecules through my false nostrils to my authentic lungs. The natives must think I'm insane. Tripping on auto exhaust! Can I get arrested for over enthusiastic public breathing? Will they pull me in for a mental checkup?

Elizabeth Cooke continues to waft wistful attentions at me. Smiles in the hallway. Hopeful gleam of the eyes. "Perhaps we can have dinner together some night soon,

Mr. Knecht. I know we'd have so much to talk about. And maybe you'd like to see the new poems I've been doing." She is trembling. Eyelids flickering tensely; head held rigid on long neck. I know she sometimes has men in her room, so it can't be out of loneliness or frustration that she's cultivating me. And I doubt that she's sexually attracted to my outer self. I believe I'm being accurate when I say that women don't consider me sexually magnetic. No, she loves me because she pities me. The sad shy bachelor at the end of the hall, dear unhappy Mr. Knecht; can I bring some brightness into his dreary life? And so forth. I think that's how it is. Will I be able to go on avoiding her? Perhaps I should move to another part of the city. But I've lived here so long; I've grown accustomed to this hotel. Its easy ways do much to compensate for the hardships of my post. And my familiar room. The huge many-paned window; the cracked green floor tiles in the bathroom; the lumpy patterns of re-plastering on the wall above my bed. The high ceiling; the funny chandelier. Things that I love. But of course I can't let her try to start an affair with me. We are supposed to observe Earthfolk, not to get involved with them. Our disguise is not that difficult to penetrate at close range. I must keep her away somehow. Or flee.

Incredible! There is another of us in this very hotel!

As I learned through accident. At one this afternoon, returning from my morning travels: Elizabeth in the lobby, as though lying in wait for me, chatting with the manager. Rides up with me in the elevator. Her eyes looking into mine. "Sometimes I think you're afraid of me," she begins. "You mustn't be. That's the great tragedy of human life, that people shut themselves up behind walls of fear and never let anyone through, anyone who might care about them and be warm to them. You've got no reason to be afraid of me." I do, but how to explain that to her? To sidestep prolonged conversation and possible entan-

glement I get off the elevator one floor below the right
one. Let her think I'm visiting a friend. Or a mistress.
I walk slowly down the hall to the stairs, using up time,
waiting so she will be in her room before I go up. A
maid bustles by me. She thrusts her key into a door on
the left: a rare *faux pas* for the usually competent help
here, she forgets to knock before going in to make up
the room. The door opens and the occupant, inside, stands
revealed. A stocky, muscular man, naked to the waist.
"Oh, excuse me," the maid gasps, and backs out, shutting
the door. But I have seen. My eyes are quick. The hairy
chest is split, a dark gash three inches wide and some
eleven inches long, beginning between the nipples and
going past the navel. Visible within is the black shiny
surface of a Homeworld carapace. My countryman,
opening up for Second Feeding. Dazed, numbed, I stag-
ger to the stairs and pull myself step by leaden step to
my floor. No sign of Elizabeth. I stumble into my room
and throw the bolt. Another of us here? Well, why not?
I'm not the only one. There may be hundreds in New
York alone. But in the same hotel? I remember, now,
I've seen him occasionally: a silent, dour man, tense,
hunted-looking, unsociable. No doubt I appear the same
way to others. Keep the world at a distance. I don't know
his name or what he is supposed to do for a living.

We are forbidden to make contact with fellow Homeworlders except in case of extreme emergency. Isolation
is a necessary condition of our employment. I may not
introduce myself to him; I may not seek his friendship.
It is worse now for me, knowing that he is here, than
when I was entirely alone. The things we could reminisce
about! The friends we might have in common! We could
reinforce one another's endurance of the gravity, the discomfort of our disguises, the vile climate. But no. I must
pretend I know nothing. The rules. The harsh, unbending
rules. I to go about my business, he his; if we meet, no

hint of my knowledge must pass.

So be it. I will honor my vows. But it may be difficult.

He goes by the name of Swanson. Been living in the hotel eighteen months; a musician of some sort, according to the manager. "A very peculiar man. Keeps to himself; no small talk, never smiles. Defends his privacy. The other day a maid barged into his room without knocking and I thought he'd sue. Well, we get all sorts here." The manager thinks he may actually be a member of one of the old European royal families, living in exile, or something similarly romantic. The manager would be surprised.

I defend my privacy too. From Elizabeth, another assault on it.

In the hall outside my room. "My new poems," she said. "In case you're interested." And then: "Can I come in? I'd read them to you. I love reading out loud." And: "Please don't always seem so terribly afraid of me. I don't bite, David. Really I don't. I'm quite gentle."

"I'm sorry."

"So am I." Anger, now, lurking in her shiny eyes, her thin taut lips. "If you want me to leave you alone, say so, I will. But I want you to know how cruel you're being. I don't *demand* anything from you. I'm just offering some friendship. And you're refusing. Do I have a bad smell? Am I so ugly? Is it my poems you hate and you're afraid to tell me?"

"Elizabeth—"

"We're only on this world such a short time. Why can't we be kinder to each other while we are? To love, to share, to open up. The reality trip. Communication, soul to soul." Her tone changed. An artful shading. "For all I know, women turn you off. I wouldn't put anybody down for that. We've all got our ways. But it doesn't have to be a sexual thing, you and me. Just talk. Like, opening the channels. Please? Say no and I'll never bother you again, but don't say no, please. That's like shutting a door on life, David. And when you do that, you start to die a little."

Persistent. I should tell her to go to hell. But there is the loneliness. There is her obvious sincerity. Her warmth, her eagerness to pull me from my lunar isolation. Can there be harm in it? Knowing that Swanson is nearby, so close yet sealed from me by iron commandments, has intensified my sense of being alone. I can risk letting Elizabeth get closer to me. It will make her happy; it may make me happy; it could even yield information valuable to Homeworld. Of course I must still maintain certain barriers.

"I don't mean to be unfriendly. I think you've mis-understood, Elizabeth. I haven't really been rejecting you. Come in. Do come in." Stunned, she enters my room. The first guest ever. My few books; my modest furnishings; the ultrawave transmitter, impenetrably disguised as a piece of sculpture. She sits. Skirt far above the knees. Good legs, if I understand the criteria of quality correctly. I am determined to allow no sexual over-tures. If she tries anything, I'll resort to—I don't know—hysteria. "Read me your new poems," I say. She opens her portfolio. Reads.

In the midst of the hipster night of doubt and
Emptiness, when the bad-trip god came to me with
Cold hands, I looked up and shouted yes at the
Stars. And yes and yes again. I groove on yes;
The devil grooves on no. And I waited for you to
Say yes, and at last you did. And the world said
The stars said the trees said the grass said the
Sky said the streets said yes and yes and yes—

She is ecstatic. Her face is flushed; her eyes are joyous. She has broken through to me. After two hours, when it becomes obvious that I am not going to ask her to go to bed with me, she leaves. Not to wear out her welcome. "I'm so glad I was wrong about you, David," she whispers. "I couldn't believe you were really a life-denier. And you're not." Ecstatic.

I am getting into very deep water.

We spend an hour or two together every night. Sometimes in my room, sometimes in hers. Usually she comes to me, but now and then, to be polite, I seek her out after Third Feeding. By now I've read all her poetry; we talk instead of the arts in general, politics, racial problems. She has a lively, well-stocked, disorderly mind. Though she probes constantly for information about me, she realizes how sensitive I am, and quickly withdraws when I parry her. Asking about my work: I reply vaguely that I'm doing research for a book, and when I don't amplify she drops it, though she tries again, gently, a few nights later. She drinks a lot of wine, and offers it to me. I nurse one glass through a whole visit. Often she suggests we go out together for dinner; I explain that I have digestive problems and prefer to eat alone, and she takes this in good grace but immediately resolves to help me overcome those problems, for soon she is asking me to eat with her again. There is an excellent Spanish restaurant right in the hotel, she says. She drops troublesome questions. Where was I born? Did I go to college? Do I have family somewhere? Have I ever been married? Have I published any of my writings? I improvise evasions. Nothing difficult about that, except that never before have I allowed anyone on Earth such sustained contact with me, so prolonged an opportunity to find inconsistencies in my pretended identity. What if she sees through?

And sex. Her invitations grow less subtle. She seems

to think that we ought to be having a sexual relationship, simply because we've become such good friends. Not a matter of passion so much as one of communication: we talk, sometimes we take walks together, we should do *that* together too. But of course it's impossible. I have the external organs but not the capacity to use them. Wouldn't want her touching my false skin in any case. How to deflect her? If I declare myself impotent she'll demand a chance to try to cure me. If I pretend homosexuality she'll start some kind of straightening therapy. If I simply say she doesn't turn me on physically she'll be hurt. The sexual thing is a challenge to her, the way merely getting me to talk with her once was. She often wears the transparent pink shawl that reveals her breasts. Her skirts are hip-high. She doses herself with aphrodisiac perfumes. She grazes my body with hers whenever opportunity arises. The tension mounts; she is determined to have me.

I have said nothing about her in my reports to Homeworld. Though I do transmit some of the psychological data I have gathered by observing her.

"Could you ever admit you were in love with me?" she asked tonight.

And she asked, "Doesn't it hurt you to repress your feelings all the time? To sit there locked up inside yourself like a prisoner?"

And, "There's a physical side of life too, David. I don't mind so much the damage you're doing to me by ignoring it. But I worry about the damage you're doing to you."

Crossing her legs. Hiking her skirt even higher.

We are heading toward a crisis. I should never have let this begin. A torrid summer has descended on the city, and in hot weather my nervous system is always at the edge of eruption. She may push me too far. I might ruin everything. I should apply for transfer to Homeworld before I cause trouble. Maybe I should confer with Swanson. I think what is happening now qualifies as an emergency.

Elizabeth stayed past midnight tonight. I had to ask her finally to leave: work to do. An hour later she pushed an envelope under my door. Newest poems. Love poems. In a shaky hand: *"David you mean so much to me. You mean the stars and nebulas. Can't you let me show my love? Can't you accept happiness? Think about it. I adore you."*

What have I started?

103°F, today. The fourth successive day of intolerable heat. Met Swanson in the elevator at lunch time; nearly blurted the truth about myself to him. I must be more careful. But my control is slipping. Last night, in the worst of the heat, I was tempted to strip off my disguise. I could no longer stand being locked in here, pivoting and ducking to avoid all the machinery festooned about me. Resisted the temptation; just barely. Somehow I am more sensitive to the gravity too. I have the illusion that my carapace is developing cracks. Almost collapsed in the street this afternoon. All I need: heat exhaustion, whisked off to the hospital, routine fluroscope exam. "You have a very odd skeletal structure, Mr. Knecht." Indeed. Dissecting me, next, with three thousand medical students looking on. And then the United Nations called in. Menace from outer space. Yes. I must be more careful. I must be more careful. I must be more—

Now I've done it. Eleven years of faithful service destroyed in a single wild moment. Violation of the Fundamental Rule. I hardly believe it. How was it possible that I—that I—with my respect for my responsibilities—that I could have—even considered, let alone actually done—

But the weather was terribly hot. The third week of the heat wave. I was stifling inside my false body. And the gravity: was New York having a gravity wave too? That terrible pull, worse than ever. Bending my internal organs out of shape. Elizabeth a tremendous annoyance: passionate, emotional, teary, poetic, giving me no rest, pleading for me to burn with a brighter flame. Declaring her love in sonnets, in rambling hip epics, in haiku. Spending two hours in my room, crouched at my feet, murmuring about the hidden beauty of my soul. "Open yourself and let love come in," she whispered. "It's like giving yourself to God. Making a commitment; breaking down all walls. Why not? For love's sake, David, why not?" I couldn't tell her why not, and she went away, but about midnight she was back knocking at my door. I let her in. She wore an ankle-length silk housecoat, gleaming, threadbare. "I'm stoned," she said hoarsely, voice an octave too deep. "I had to bust three joints to get up the nerve. But here I am. David, I'm sick of making the turnoff trip. We've been so wonderfully close, and then you won't go the last stretch of the way." A cascade of giggles. "Tonight you will. Don't fail me. Darling." Drops the housecoat. Naked underneath it; narrow waist, bony hips, long legs, thin thighs, blue veins crossing her breasts. Her hair wild and kinky. A sorceress. A seeress. Berserk. Approaching me, eyes slit-wide, mouth open, tongue flickering snakily. How fleshless how she is! Beads of sweat glistening on her flat chest. Seizes my wrists; tugs me roughly toward the bed. We tussle a little. Within my false body I throw switches, nudge levers. I am stronger than she is. I pull free, breaking her hold with an effort. She stands flat-footed in front of me, glaring, eyes fiery. So vulnerable, so sad in her nudity. And yet so fierce. "David! David! David!" Sobbing. Breathless. Pleading with her eyes and the tips of her breasts. Gathering her strength; now she makes the next lunge, but I see it coming and let her topple past me. She lands on the bed, burying her face in the pillow, clawing at the sheet. "Why? Why why why WHY?" she screams.

In a minute we will have the manager in here. With the police.

"Am I so hideous? I love you, David, do you know what that word means? Love. Love." Sits up. Turns to me. Imploring. "Don't reject me," she whispers. "I couldn't take that. You know, I just wanted to make you happy, I figured I could be the one, only I didn't realize how unhappy you'd make me. And you just stand there. And you don't say anything. What are you, some kind of machine?"

"I'll tell you what I am," I said.

That was when I went sliding into the abyss. All control lost; all prudence gone. My mind so slathered with raw emotion that survival itself means nothing. I must make things clear to her, is all. I must show her. At whatever expense. I strip off my shirt. She glows, no doubt thinking I will let myself be seduced. My hands slide up and down my bare chest, seeking the catches and snaps. I go through the intricate, cumbersome process of opening my body. Deep within myself something is shouting NO NO NO NO NO, but I pay no attention. The heart has its reasons.

Hoarsely: "Look, Elizabeth. Look at me. This is what I am. Look at me and freak out. The reality trip."

My chest opens wide.

I push myself forward, stepping between the levers and struts, emerging halfway from the human shell I wear. I have not been this far out of it since the day they sealed me in, on Homeworld. I let her see my gleaming carapace. I wave my eyestalks around. I allow some of my claws to show. "See? See? Big black crab from outer space. That's what you love, Elizabeth. That's what I am. David Knecht's just a costume, and this is what's inside it." I have gone insane. "You want reality? Here's reality,

Elizabeth. What good is the Knecht body to you? It's a fraud. It's a machine. Come on, come closer. Do you want to kiss me? Should I get on you and make love?"

During this episode her face has displayed an amazing range of reactions. Open-mouthed disbelief at first, of course. And frozen horror: gagging sounds in throat, jaws agape, eyes wide and rigid. Hands fanned across breasts. Suddenly modesty in front of the alien monster? But then, as the familiar Knecht-voice, now bitter and impassioned, continues to flow from the black thing within the sundered chest, a softening of her response. Curiosity. The poetic sensibility taking over. Nothing human is alien to me: Terence, quoted by Cicero. Nothing alien is alien to me. Eh? She will accept the evidence of her eyes. "What are you? Where did you come from?" And I say, "I've violated the Fundamental Rule. I deserve to be plucked and thinned. We're not supposed to reveal ourselves. If we get into some kind of accident that might lead to exposure, we're supposed to blow ourselves up. The switch is right here." She comes close and peers around me, into the cavern of David Knecht's chest. "From some other planet? Living here in disguise?" She understands the picture. Her shock is fading. She even laughs. "I've seen worse than you on acid," she says. "You don't frighten me now, David. David? Shall I go on calling you David?"

This is unreal and dreamlike to me. I have revealed myself, thinking to drive her away in terror; she is no longer aghast, and smiles at my strangeness. She kneels to get a better look. I move back a short way. Eyestalks fluttering: I am uneasy, I have somehow lost the upper hand in this encounter.

She says, "I knew you were unusual, but not like this. But it's all right. I can cope. I mean, the essential personality, that's what I fell in love with. Who cares that you're a crabman from the Green Galaxy? Who cares that we can't ever be real lovers? I can make that sacrifice. It's your soul I dig, David. Go on. Close yourself up again. You don't look comfortable this way." The triumph of love. She will not abandon me, even now. Disaster. I crawl back into Knecht and lift his arms to his chest to seal it. Shock is glazing my consciousness: the enormity, the audacity. What have I done? Elizabeth watches, awed, even delighted. At last I am together again. She nods. "Listen," she tells me, "you can trust me. I mean, if you're some kind of spy, checking out the Earth, I don't care. *I don't care*. I won't tell anybody. Pour it all out, David. Tell me about yourself. Don't you see, this is the biggest thing that ever happened to me. A chance to show that love isn't just physical, isn't just chemistry, that it's a soul trip, that it crosses not just racial lines but the lines of the whole damned species, the planet itself—"

It took several hours to get rid of her. A soaring, intense conversation, Elizabeth doing most of the talking. She putting forth theories of why I had come to Earth, me nodding, denying, amplifying, mostly lost in horror at my own perfidy and barely listening to her monologue. And the humidity turning me into rotting rags. Finally: "I'm down from the pot, David. And all wound up. I'm going out for a walk. Then back to my room to write for a while. To put this night into a poem before I lose the power of it. But I'll come to you again by dawn, all right? That's maybe five hours from now. You'll be here? You won't do anything foolish? Oh, I love you so much, David! Do you believe me? Do you?"

When she was gone I stood a long while by the window, trying to reassemble myself. Shattered. Drained. Remembering her kisses, her lips running along the ridge marking the place where my chest opens. The fascination of the abomination. She will love me even if I am crustaceous beneath.

I had to have help.

I went to Swanson's room. He was slow to respond to my knock; busy transmitting, no doubt. I could hear him within, but he didn't answer. "Swanson?" I called. "Swanson?" Then I added the distress signal in the Homeworld tongue. He rushed to the door. Blinking, suspicious. "It's all right," I said. "Look, let me in. I'm in big trouble." Speaking English, but I gave him the distress signal again.

"How did you know about me?" he asked.

"The day the maid blundered into your room while you were eating, I was going by. I saw."

"But you aren't supposed to—"

"Except in emergencies. This is an emergency." He shut off his ultrawave and listened intently to my story. Scowling. He didn't approve. But he wouldn't spurn me. I had been criminally foolish, but I was of his kind, prey to the same pains, the same lonelinesses, and he would help me.

"What do you plan to do now?" he asked. "You can't harm her. It isn't allowed."

"I don't want to harm her. Just to get free of her. To make her fall out of love with me."

"How? If showing yourself to her didn't—"

"Infidelity," I said. "Making her see that I love someone else. No room in my life for her. That'll drive her away. Afterwards it won't matter that she knows: who'd believe her story? The FBI would laugh and tell her to lay off the LSD. But if I don't break her attachment to me I'm finished."

"Love someone else? Who?"

"When she comes back to my room at dawn," I said, "she'll find the two of us together, dividing and abstracting. I think that'll do it; don't you?"

So I deceived Elizabeth with Swanson.

The fact that we both wore male human identities was

irrelevant, of course. We went to my room and stepped out of our disguises—a bold, dizzying sensation!—and suddenly we were just two Homeworlders again, receptive to one another's needs. I left the door unlocked. Swanson and I crawled up on my bed and began the chanting. How strange it was, after these years of solitude, to feel those vibrations again! And how beautiful. Swanson's vibrissae touching mine. The interplay of harmonies. An underlying sternness to his technique—he was contemptuous of me for my idiocy, and rightly so— but once we passed from the chanting to the dividing all was forgiven, and as we moved into the abstracting it was truly sublime. We climbed through an infinity of climactic emptyings. Dawn crept upon us and found us unwilling to halt even for rest.

A knock at the door. Elizabeth.

"Come in," I said.

A dreamy, ecstatic look on her face. Fading instantly when she saw the two of us entangled on the bed. A questioning frown. "We've been mating," I explained. "Did you think I was a complete hermit?" She looked from Swanson to me, from me to Swanson. Hand over her mouth. Eyes anguished. I turned the screw a little tighter. "I couldn't stop you from falling in love with me, Elizabeth. But I really do prefer my own kind. As should have been obvious."

"To have her here now, though—when you knew I was coming back—"

"Not *her,* exactly. Not *him* exactly either, though,"

"—so cruel, David! To ruin such a beautiful experience." Holding forth sheets of paper with shaking hands. "A whole sonnet cycle," she said. "About tonight. How beautiful it was, and all. And now—and now—" Crumpling the pages. Hurling them across the room. Turning. Running out, sobbing furiously. Hell hath no fury like. *"David!"* A smothered cry. And slamming the door.

* * *

She was back in ten minutes. Swanson and I hadn't quite finished donning our bodies yet; we were both still unsealed. As we worked, we discussed further steps to take: he felt honor demanded that I request a transfer back to Homeworld, having terminated my usefulness here through tonight's indiscreet revelation. I agreed with him to some degree but was reluctant to leave. Despite the bodily torment of life on Earth I had come to feel I belonged here. Then Elizabeth entered, radiant.

"I mustn't be so possessive," she announced. "So bourgeois. So conventional. I'm willing to share my love." Embracing Swanson. Embracing me. "A *ménage à trois*," she said. "I won't mind that you two are having a physical relationship. As long as you don't shut me out of your lives completely. I mean, David, we could never have been physical anyway, right, but we can have the other aspects of love, and we'll open ourselves to your friend also. Yes? Yes? Yes?"

Swanson and I both put in applications for transfer, he to Africa, me to Homeworld. It would be some time before we received a reply. Until then we were at her mercy. He was blazingly angry with me for involving him in this, but what choice had I had? Nor could either of us avoid Elizabeth. We were at her mercy. She bathed both of us in shimmering waves of tender emotion; wherever we turned, there she was, incandescent with love. Lighting up the darkness of our lives. You poor lonely creatures. Do you suffer much in our gravity? What about the heat? And the winters. Is there a custom of marriage on your planet? Do you have poetry?

A happy threesome. We went to the theatre together. To concerts. Even to parties in Greenwich Village. "My friends," Elizabeth said, leaving no doubt in anyone's mind that she was living with both of us. Faintly scandalous doings; she loved to seem daring. Swanson was

sullenly obliging, putting up with her antics but privately
haranguing me for subjecting him to all this. Elizabeth
got out another mimeographed booklet of poems, dedicated to both of us. *Triple Tripping,* she called it. Fla-
grantly erotic. I quoted a few of the poems in one of my
reports to Homeworld, then lost heart and hid the booklet
in the closet. "Have you heard about your transfer yet?"
I asked Swanson at least twice a week. He hadn't. Neither
had I.

Autumn came. Elizabeth, burning her candle at both
ends, looked gaunt and feverish. "I have never known
such happiness," she announced frequently, one hand
clasping Swanson, the other me. "I never think about
the strangeness of you anymore. I think of you only as
people. Sweet, wonderful, lonely people. Here in the
darkness of this horrid city." And she once said, "What
if everybody here is like you, and I'm the only one who's
really human? But that's silly. You must be the only ones
of your kind here. The advance scouts. Will your planet
invade ours? I do hope so! Set everything to rights. The
reign of love and reason at last!"

"How long will this go on?" Swanson muttered.

At the end of October his transfer came through. He left
without saying goodbye to either of us and without
leaving a forwarding address. Nairobi? Addis Ababa?
Kinshasa?

I had grown accustomed to having him around to share
the burden of Elizabeth. Now the full brunt of her af-
fection fell on me. My work was suffering; I had no time
to file my reports properly. And I lived in fear of her
gossiping. What was she telling her Village friends? ("You
know David? He's not really a man, you know. Actually
inside him there's a kind of crab-thing from another solar
system. But what does that matter? Love's a universal
phenomenon. The truly loving person doesn't draw limits

around the planet.") I longed for my release. To go home; to accept my punishment; to shed my false skin. To empty my mind of Elizabeth.

My reply came through the ultrawave on November 13. Application denied. I was to remain on Earth and continue my work as before. Transfers to Homeworld were granted only for reasons of health.

I debated sending a full account of my treason to Homeworld and thus bringing about my certain recall. But I hesitated, overwhelmed with despair. Dark brooding seized me. "Why so sad?" Elizabeth asked. What could I say? That my attempt at escaping from her had failed? "I love you," she said. "I've never felt so *real* before." Nuzzling against my cheek. Fingers knotted in my hair. A seductive whisper. "David, open yourself up again. Your chest, I mean. I want to see the inner you. To make sure I'm not frightened of it. Please? You've only let me see you once." And then, when I had: "May I kiss you, David?" I was appalled. But I let her. She was unafraid. Transfigured by happiness. She is a cosmic nuisance, but I fear I'm getting to like her.

Can I leave her? I wish Swanson had not vanished. I need advice.

Either I break with Elizabeth or I break with Homeworld. This is absurd. I find new chasms of despondency every day. I am unable to do my work. I have requested a transfer once again, without giving details. The first snow of the winter today.

Application denied.

"When I found you with Swanson," she said, "it was a terrible shock. An even bigger blow than when you first came out of your chest. I mean, it was startling to find out you weren't human, but it didn't hit me in any emotional way, it didn't threaten me. But then, to come back a few hours later and find you with one of your own kind, to know that you wanted to shut me out, that I had no place in your life—Only we worked it out, didn't we?" Kissing me. Tears of joy in her eyes. How did this happen? Where did it all begin? Existence was once so simple. I have tried to trace the chain of events that brought me from there to here, and I cannot. I was outside of my false body for eight hours today. The longest spell so far. Elizabeth is talking of going to the islands with me for the winter. A secluded cottage that her friends will make available. Of course, I must not leave my post without permission. And it takes months simply to get a reply.

Let me admit the truth: I love her.

January 1. The new year begins. I have sent my resignation to Homeworld and have destroyed my ultrawave equipment. The links are broken. Tomorrow, when the city offices are open, Elizabeth and I will go to get the marriage license.

THE SHRINES OF EARTH

Master-poet Jorun Kedrik looked up at the nearly flawless blue sky and said, "Earth's a lovely world. It would be a pity if the Hrossai conquered it, wouldn't it?"

He was lying on a greenswarded, gently sloping hill just outside his current dwelling near ancient Paris. Earth no longer had cities, and nothing remained of old Paris, nothing but the one monstrosity of iron strutworks jutting nearly a thousand feet into the air half a mile away. Even at this distance, Kedrik's keen eyes picked out the bright robes of some tourists from New Gallia who were re-visiting their ancestral shrine.

At his side, his companion, musician-apprentice Levri Amsler, was stretched face-down on the grass. Amsler, long-legged, angular-featured, said, "How certain is the invasion? When's it due?"

Kedrik shrugged. "Five years, six, maybe. Our best sociologists worked out the projection. The Hrossai will be coming down out of the Centauri system, and the first stop is Earth. It makes a convenient jumping-off point for their conquest of the galaxy."

"And they know they can knock us over without a fight," Amsler added mournfully. He rolled over, picked up his flute, and brushed a few strands of grass away from the mouthpiece. Pursing his lips, he played a brief, poignant melody, ending in a striking minor cadence.

"Nicely conceived," Kedrik said approvingly. "Perhaps the Hrossai will keep us alive as court musicians— you, at least." Then he chuckled harshly. "No, that's not likely. There's little place in their scheme of things for flute players or poets. They'll be looking for soldiers."

"They won't find any here," the younger man said, putting down the flute. "There isn't a man on Earth who'd know which end of a gun to point if a Hross gave it to him."

Kedrik rose and stretched. "Three thousand years of peace! Three thousand years of contentment! Well, it couldn't last forever, Levri. We were once the galaxy's fiercest fighters; if we want to survive the Hrossai onslaught, we'll have to relearn some of our ancient skills."

"No! Warfare, on Earth—again?" Amsler asked. "I'd almost think it would be better to let the Hrossai destroy us, you know?"

"Faulty thinking," Kedrik said testily. "Contrasurvival. Gutless. Foolish."

"What do you mean?"

"We were once the galaxy's most ruthless killers, when we needed to be," Kedrik said. "In the old days, we made the grubby little Hrossai look like saints." He grinned and added, "But we were also the galaxy's shrewdest intriguers. And *that's* a skill we haven't forgotten, I'd say."

"What's on your mind, Jorun?"

"You'll see. Come: let's amble over to yonder ugly pile of metal and chat with those tourists from New Gallia. They always welcome a chance to gawk at the quaint pastoral types that inhabit their mother world."

* * *

New Gallia was a large, cheerful planet in the Albireo system. Lit by a double star, fifth-magnitude blue and third-magnitude yellow, the colony never lacked for sunlight of one color or another; the brighter yellow sun supplied most of the heat, the fifth-magnitude blue providing that extra touch of color, the decorative flair, that the New Gallians loved so dearly.

New Gallia had been the second extrasolar planet to be settled by Terran colonists, during the years of the great exodus. The *Jules Verne* had brought five hundred hand-picked couples there in 2316, ten years after the United States had planted its colony, Columbia, in the Sirius system, and five years before the *Boris Godunov* deposited its cargo of ex-Muscovites on the steps of Novaya Ruthenia, formerly Procyon VI.

The current Chief of State on New Gallia was a slim, dark-complected mathematician named Justin LeFebvre, whose term of office, barring a collapse of the government, had still eight months to go. LeFebvre would have loved nothing more greatly than the overthrow of his government; he longed to rid himself of the tiresome job and return to Theory of Sets.

But duty was duty, and *someone* had to do the job. Furthermore, pride was pride. It was a point of honor for a New Gallian premier to survive in office for the duration of a full one-year term, and much as he hated the job, LeFebvre privately was doing his best not to lose it.

In his office on the seventy-second floor of the Bastille—named for some forgotten, legend-shrouded building of Earth—LeFebvre stared at the excited-looking man before him.

Frowning, the Chief of State said, "Slowly, my good man, slowly! Begin from the beginning, and tell me exactly what you heard, M. Dauzat."

M. Dauzat, a wealthy beet-farmer who had held the premiership a decade before, forced himself into a state of calm. "Very well, sir. As I said: my wife and I had decided at last to visit Earth, to see our ancestral world, the mother of our people. And, naturally, to pay our respects at the Tower."

"Naturally."

"We were, then, at the very base of the Tower, preparing to make the ascent, when a pair of natives approached us. Like all native Terrans, they were charming, simple people; they wore cloaks of gentle hues, carried musical instruments, and spoke in even more musical tones. Mme. Dauzat was quite taken with them."

"Of course," LeFebvre said impatiently. Now that he had slowed Dauzat down, there seemed to be no way of accelerating the pace of the narrative again. "We all know how charming the Terrans are. But go on."

"To be brief, we invited them to make the ascent of the Tower with us. We reached the top and gazed out over the peaceful green land that had once been France"—an expansive smile spread over Dauzat's heavy jowls—"and then the older of the two Terrans said, in a voice muffled with sadness, that it was indeed a misfortune that the uncultured savages from Columbia planned to destroy our noble Tower."

"What?"

LeFebvre paled; he rose stiffly from his webchair and stared in horror at Dauzat. "Would you say that again, M. Dauzat?"

"I only repeat what the native told me. He informed me that it was generally feared that Columbia intended to destroy the Tower, as the first step in a possible campaign planned at beginning open war between our worlds."

"I see," LeFebvre said numbly.

Relations between New Gallia and the American-settled planet Columbia had been, to say the least, strained, during the past four centuries—and only the instance of Novaya Ruthenia, the third major power in the galaxy, had kept the French and American colonies from war.

Right now, Novaya Ruthenia and New Gallia were enjoying uneasy "friendly relations," with each other, and both were on the outs with the Columbians. But in a war between New Gallia and Columbia, the Ruthenians would be sure to profit; the eager Russians would be quick to gobble up the best trade routes to such minor neutral worlds as Xanadu and Britannia.

But still, an attack on the Tower, the symbol and focal point of New Gallic life—! *Sacre bleu*, it was provocation for war!

Nodding to the fat man, LeFebvre said, *"Merci*, M. Dauzat. Your thoughtfulness in cutting short your vacation to return here with this disturbing news will not go unappreciated."

"I would have communicated with you direct," said Dauzat. "But the subradio channels are so uncertain, and I feared interception."

"You acted rightly, *M'sieu."* LeFebvre pushed the communicator stud on his desk and said, "An immediate Council meeting is called, top priority. Everyone is to be here. *Everyone."*

"The Radical ministers are holding a party caucus, M. LeFebvre," his secretary's emotionless voice informed him. "Shall I contact them?"

"By all means. Their caucus is of no importance now." Hoarsely he added, "Besides, they may be back in power by nightfall anyway. Only don't tell them that."

"Order, please, gentlemen. Order!"

LeFebvre pushed away the sheet of paper on which he had been calming himself with quadratics, and said once again, *"Order!"*

The room quieted. Seated to his left were seven ministers of his party, the Social Conservatives; to his right were the three Democratic Radical men he had chosen to include in his coalition government, plus four more Dem-Rads of high party standing but noncabinet status.

He had invited them for the sake of equality; a crisis of this sort transcended mere party barriers.

"You've heard the story substantially as M. Dauzat gave it to me. Now, we all know and trust M. Dauzat— while those Terrans, of course, being inhabitants of France herself, were certainly telling the truth. Before we proceed, gentlemen, I'd like to call for a cabinet vote of confidence; I'll resign if it's your will."

The vote was seven for LeFebvre, three against. LeFebvre remained in office.

"Now, then. We're faced with the prospect of an attack on the Eiffel Tower itself, as the opening move in a war Columbia is obviously planning to declare. Are there any suggestions?"

M. de Villefosse, Secretary of Interworld Affairs, leaned forward and said, "Certainly. We must arm ourselves at once, and prepare for this war!"

M. Raval, Secretary of Home Defense, said, "A good thought! We hold our ships in readiness, and strike at Columbia the instant the Tower is attacked. We could also, in retaliation, destroy the Columbians' own shrine on Earth."

"The Washington Monument?" said M. Bournon, Secretary of Culture. "But why wipe out two monuments? Why not simply establish a guard over our own?"

"The Terrans would not care for an armed enclave of our men on their territory," LeFebvre pointed out. "They might protest. They might enlist the aid of the Ruthenians, and then we'd face attack from both sides." The Premier's fingers trembled; he had never anticipated a crisis of this magnitude.

"I have the solution, then," announced M. de Simon, the Democratic-Radical Secretary of the Economy. "We establish a permanent guard force in space, in constant orbit around Earth. Our ships will remain forever on the lookout for this attack from Columbia, and will be ready to defend our Tower when the time comes."

"An excellent suggestion," said LeFebvre. "The Earthmen won't object—I hope—and we won't be transgressing on anyone's national boundaries. We will, though, be able to defend the Tower. I call for a vote."

The vote was unanimous—the first time the New Gallian cabinet had so quickly agreed on anything in 384 years.

Deciding on the number of ships to be sent was a different matter. It took six hours, but at the end of that time it was officially determined that nine New Gallian ships of the line were to be sent to Earth as a defensive force, to protect New Gallia's most sacred shrine.

Premier LeFebvre slept soundly that night, dreaming of surds and integrals. The crisis was averted—or, at least, postponed. The government had not fallen. And, *le bon Dieu* grant it, Columbia would not decide to start its war for at least eight months, by which time LeFebvre would be a private citizen once again.

Pyotr Alexandrovitch Miaskovski, Acting Czar of all Novaya Ruthenia, squinted myopically at the slip of paper in his stubby fingers, and sighed.

It was a report from one of the Ruthenian scouts who patrolled the sector of the galaxy that included Sol. The dispatch had just come in, over tight-beam subradio direct from the vicinity of Pluto. It said:

TO: Acting Czar Pyotr Alexandrovitch
FROM: Major-Colonel Ilya Tarantyev, First Scout Squadron.

Excellency:

A fleet of nine New Gallian vessels observed taking up orbits round Sol III. They seemed armed. They appear to be preparing for large-scale military enterprise. Please advise.

Miaskovski fingered the dispatch, made a sour face, and tapped his thumbs together unhappily. Somewhere, elsewhere in the royal palace, Czar Alexei lay peacefully sleeping, far removed from worldly cares.

Bozhe moi! Miaskovski thought dismally. The New Gallians were taking position around Earth? *Why?* Did this presage a war, a breaking down of the uneasy balance of power that had held between the three major worlds for so long?

And why did it have to happen now—now, when the Czar lay wrapped in impenetrable catatonia and the cares of the state devolved upon *him?*

Miaskovski squared his shoulders. An election was scheduled for the following week, to choose the successor to Alexei. Miaskovski had been planning to run. He didn't intend to let a minor crisis like this upset his ambitions.

He flicked on the visiscreen, and the square-set, pudgy face of his secretary appeared.

"Olga, have the Ambassador from New Gallia sent here at once, will you?"

"Certainly, Excellency. At once."

Miaskovski broke the circuit and sat back in his heavy chair. *Uneasy lies the head,* he thought—but the Czarship was a coveted plum despite the headaches. His handling of this situation would help to sway the electorate next week, he hoped.

"You wish to see me, Czar Pyotr?"

He looked up. The lean face of Ambassador Selevine gleamed at him from the door visor.

"Ah—yes. Come in, please, M. Selevine."

The door slid back and the New Gallian diplomat entered—dressed impeccably, as always. Pyotr felt a certain sense of inferiority; his thick, coarse garments appeared crude compared with the diplomatic costume the New Gallian affected.

The Acting Czar leaned back in his big chair, coughed,

and said, "I'll be very blunt with you, M. Selevine. I want an explanation of this situation." He handed the New Gallian the scout's dispatch.

"But of course, Your Majesty."

Selevine took the sheet and scanned it rapidly. Miaskovski watched closely; the diplomat appeared to be somewhat ruffled.

Selevine folded the paper neatly in half and placed it on the Czar's desk. He smiled coldly, revealing perfect white teeth.

"Nine ships," he remarked idly.

"Ahem—yes. Nine ships. Does your government have any official explanation of this sudden entry into a neutral area?"

Selevine's smile vanished. "We do. The maneuver is strictly a defensive one, with no hostile intent whatever."

"Defensive? How so?"

"Be assured that the Free World of Novaya Ruthenia is not concerned in the matter, Czar Pyotr. It is strictly a matter between us and—and another planet, Your Majesty."

"Oh?" One of Pyotr's bushy eyebrows rose. "Would you care to expand on that theme, M. Selevine?"

The diplomat grinned frigidly. "One of my world's most revered shrines is located on Earth, Czar Pyotr. I refer, of course, to the Eiffel Tower. We—ah—have been given to understand that a rival power in the galaxy has designs against this shrine of ours, for motives that are not yet clear to us. We are merely taking precautions."

"You mean that the Columbians are planning to blast your damned tower?" Pyotr asked in surprise.

"I mentioned no world specifically, Excellency."

"Ah—of course."

The Acting Czar scratched his forehead for a moment, squinting surreptitiously at the New Gallian and trying without success to peer behind his diplomatic mask. "Very well, then," Pyotr said finally. "If I have your assurance that your world plans no hostile action against Novaya Ruthenia—"

"You have that assurance, Your Majesty."

"Then we can consider the matter no concern of Novaya Ruthenia's, or of mine. Good day, M. Selevine."

"Good day, Your Majesty. And kindly accept my best wishes for the forthcoming election."

"Ah—certainly. Thank you very much, M. Selevine."

When the diplomat had left, Miaskovski leaned back, frowning, and stared at the textured stucco of the ceiling, sorting out what he had learned.

Columbia planned an attack on the Eiffel Tower. The New Gallians were establishing a defensive fleet to prevent that. Well, that made sense.

But Novaya Ruthenia had a shrine on earth too: the heavy-walled Kremlin, relic of the long-forgotten empire called Russia. Much as the Ruthenians wished to repudiate their undemocratic past, they yet revered the massive buildings of the Kremlin. What if the Columbians planned an attack on that? Or suppose these New Gallian ships had some hidden idea? It wouldn't sit well with the people—not at all. Assuming he were elected, his reign as Czar would be brief.

Fight fire with fire, Miakovski thought.

"I want to talk to the Commissar of Security," he barked into the visiscreen.

And when the flat-featured face of Onegin, Commissar of Security, appeared on the screen, Czar Pyotr said, "Can you spare ten warships at once, Porfiry Mikheitch?"

The Commissar looked startled. "I—I suppose so, Majesty. But—"

"Good. I want ten fully armed warships sent to the Sol sector at once. They're to be placed in orbit around Sol III—Earth—with an eye toward guarding against a possible New Gallian or Columbian attack on the Kremlin. And make sure your commanders know that this is strictly a defensive maneuver!"

"Certainly, Majesty," the Commissar said in a weak voice. "I'll tend to it at once."

There was a hubbub in the office of James Edgerly, President of the Republic of Columbia. Edgerly himself, a tall, spare man in his early eighties, prematurely greyed around the temples, stood at the center of the commotion, while assorted members of his staff tried to make themselves heard over each other's shouts.

"Quiet!" Edgerly finally roared. *"Shut up!"*

That did it. The President glared belligerently around the room and said, "All right. Let's hear those reports one at a time. McMahon, you're first."

The Chief of Intelligence smiled dourly. "Yessir. As I think you may know, Mr. President, we picked up a subradio message from a Russian—I mean Ruthenian— scout last week. The message said the scout had discovered nine New Gallian ships in orbit around Earth. Later a couple of Columbian tourists visiting ancient America confirmed this. They even saw one of the New Gallian ships circle the Washington Monument and disappear in the direction of the Atlantic."

"Fill me in on the Atlantic," President Edgerly ordered.

An aide named Goodman whose job this was immediately recited, "The Atlantic is the ocean separating the Eastern from the Western Hemispheres. America is at one side, and Europe on the other."

"Okay." Edgerly turned to Sheldrick, the Chief of Security. "Give me the scout report now, Sheldrick."

"Well, sir, as soon as we intercepted the message from that Ruthenian scout, I ordered a couple of our ships into the area to take a look. And sure enough, nine New Gallian ships were lined up in a neat little ring around Earth!"

Edgerly nodded. "That all?"

"No, sir. This morning my scout force reported that

ten more ships have taken positions around the planet!"

"Ships of New Gallia?"

"Ruthenian ones, sir."

Edgerly moistened his lips and looked around the room, at the hodgepodge of Cabinet members, Congressional leaders, presidential aides, military men. He wouldn't have been at all surprised to learn that a couple of newsmen had sneaked into the conference too.

"Nine New Gallian ships, ten Ruthenian ones," he repeated. "Just hanging up there in orbit? Not doing anything?"

"That's right, sir."

"Okay. Scram, all of you! This is a serious matter, and it has to be dealt with at once." He glanced at his watch. The time was 1300. Figure two hours for preparing his speech, he thought.

"You can announce that I'll address a special joint session of Congress at 1500 sharp," the President said.

Congress assembled. Congress listened. And when President Edgerly demanded special power to deal with the crisis, Congress gave it to him.

"It's not that I'm anxious to plunge this world into war," he said ringingly. "But Columbia's pride must be upheld! Two alien powers are menacing the planet from which our ancestors sprang, the planet on which the finest form of government known to man evolved."

Applause.

"Many of us have visited Earth," Edgerly continued. "Many of us have stood before the gleaming shaft of marble that symbolizes for us the nation of our ancestors, the nation whose democratic traditions we uphold today. I speak, of course of the Washington Monument."

Thunderous applause.

"This very moment, ships of alien worlds fly over Earth. Their reason for this occupation we have not yet determined; at present, their intent is unknown. But Columbia must not remain asleep! Our ships must be present there, too!"

Wild applause.

"It may be that the worlds of New Gallia and Novaya Ruthenia plan to coalesce against us; it may be that their aims are wholly peaceful. Perhaps our shrine on Earth will be destroyed—but it will not be destroyed with impunity!"

A standing ovation followed.

That evening, thirteen WZ-1 warp-drive warships left Columbia, armed to the teeth. The Columbians were determined to see at close range just what devious plans the foreigners were laying.

The Hrossai, who lived on the fourth world of Alpha Centauri, were a race of beetle-browed humanoids with dull, smouldering eyes and flaky greyish skin. As one of the few intelligent races of nonhumans in the galaxy, they were objects of a certain amount of mild curiosity, but no one paid much attention to their activities.

A team of Terran sociologists had studied them, and had prepared an interesting report on their characteristics and attitudes. The report was even more interesting when it was projected five or six years into the future—but, naturally, the Terrans never bothered to show the report to any authorities on Columbia, New Gallia, or Novaya Ruthenia. They wouldn't have taken it very seriously anyway; the Terrans were good flute players and wrote some passable poetry, but their "science" was considered beneath contempt throughout the galaxy.

So when the Hrossai began their drive for galactic empire, the Terrans were the only ones who anticipated the attack. And Terra—the only prepared world—was the first to be assaulted.

The Hrossai, figuring the gentle people of Earth for a soft touch, sent only ten ships, and thought they were being extravagant at that.

But Terra was guarded—and had been for four years—

by thirty-two fully armed warships, each manned by a
crew made trigger-happy by four years of political friction and nerve-grinding inaction.

"It was a short war," Jorun Kedrik remarked. He and
his companion Amsler had taken a transatlantic jaunt just
after the brief, spectacular duel in the skies, and now
were staring upward at the towering bulk of the Washington Monument.

Amsler chuckled. "Shortest war on record, I'll bet. It
couldn't have taken more than ten minutes for our pro-
tectors to destroy the Hrossai ships, eh?"

"Hmm. Yes," Kedrik said. He studied the contours
of the needle of marble before him. "It's certainly prettier
than the Eiffel, anyway."

"Huh?"

"Just uttering esthetic judgments, that's all." He
grinned. "You'll have to admit the plan worked out perfectly, though. If we had appealed to any of the three
colonies for help, they would have shrugged it off—or
they might have sent a ship or two. But by shifting
emphasis to their holy places, and by playing them off
against each other, we managed to get a first-rate little
space navy, free of charge! You know, Earth beat the
Hrossai without ever firing a single shot?"

A tiny dot of black appeared against the bright blue
far above them—and, as the sun's rays struck it, it glittered.

"What's that?" Amsler asked.

"Probably a Columbian ship, guarding the Monument
from Ruthenian attack," Kedrik said. "The saps *still*
haven't caught wise, and I guess they're going to protect
us forever. Well, it's simpler than maintaining fleets of
our own, I suppose."

"Hey, mind if I snap a few photos?" a loud, rasping
voice shouted suddenly.

The two Earthmen turned toward the newcomer. He
was a tourist, broad, bulky, and heavily tanned—ob-

viously a Columbian come to visit the Monument. He was waving a complex-looking stereocam at them.

"Shall we?" Amsler asked doubtfully.

"Of course! The tourist wants a few snapshots of us simple native folk. Why shouldn't we oblige him, so he'll have a record of our primitive pastoral ways?"

Kedrik started to laugh, and after a moment Amsler joined in.

The Columbian drew near, focusing his camera. "What's the joke?" he asked. "What's so funny?"

"Nothing," Kedrik gasped between chuckles. "Just— an old Terran joke. Very obscure. You wouldn't get it."

"I'll bet the joke's on me," the tourist said good-naturedly. "Well, I don't care. Would you mind standing over there, by the Monument? It'll make a nice shot to show back home."

BLACK IS BEAUTIFUL

My nose is flat my lips are thick my hair is frizzy my
skin is black
   is beautiful
   is black is beautiful
   I am James Shabazz age seventeen born august 13
1983 I am black I am afro I am beautiful this machine
writes my words as I speak them and the machine is
black
   is beautiful

Elijah Muhammad's *The Supreme Wisdom* says:

> *Separation of the so-called Negroes from their
> slavemasters' children is a MUST. It is the only SO-
> LUTION to our problem. It was the only solution,
> according to the Bible, for Israel and the Egyptians,
> and it will prove to be the only solution for America
> and her slaves, whom she mockingly calls her citizens,
> without granting her citizenship. We must keep this in*

*our minds at all times that we are actually being
mocked.*

Catlike, moving as a black panther would, James Shabazz stalked through the city. It was late summer, and
the pumps were working hard, sucking the hot air out
from under the Manhattan domes and squirting it into
the suburbs. There had been a lot of grinding about that
lately. Whitey out there complained that all that hot air
was wilting his lawns and making his own pumps work
too hard. Screw Whitey, thought James Shabazz pleasantly. Let his lawns wilt. Let him complain. Let him get
black in the face with complaining. Do the mother some
good.

Silently, pantherlike, down Fifth Avenue to 53rd, across
to Park, down Park to 48th. Just looking around. A big
boy, sweatshiny, black but not black enough to suit him.
He wore a gaudy five-colored dashiki, beads from Mali,
flowing white belled trousers, a neat goatee, a golden
earring. In his left rear pocket: a beat-up copy of the new
novel about Malcolm. In his right rear pocket: a cute
little sonic blade.

Saturday afternoon and the air was quiet. None of the
hopterbuses coming through the domes and dumping
Whitey onto the rooftops. They stayed home today, the
commuters, the palefaces. Saturday and Sunday, the city
was black. Likewise all the other days of the week after
four P.M. Run, Whitey, Run! See Whitey run! Why does
Whitey run? Because he don't belong here no more.

Sorry, teach. I shouldn't talk like that no more, huh?

James Shabazz smiled. The identity card in his pocket
called him James Lincoln, but when he walked alone
through the city he spurned that name. The slavemaster
name. His parents stuck with it, proud of it, telling him
that no black should reject a name like Lincoln. The
dumb geeps! What did they think, that great-great-

grandpappy was owned by Honest Abe? Lincoln was a tag some belching hillbilly stuck on the family a hundred fifty years ago. If anyone asks me today, I'm James Shabazz. Black. Proud of it.

Black faces mirrored him on every street. Toward him came ten diplomats in tribal robes, not Afros but Africans, a bunch of Yorubas, Ibos, Baules, Mandingos, Ashantis, Senufos, Bakongos, Balubas, who knew what, the real thing, anyway, black as night, so black they looked purple. No slavemaster blood in them! James Shabazz smiled, nodded. Good afternoon, brothers. Nice day! They took no notice of him, but swept right on, their conversation unbroken. They were not speaking Swahili, which he would have recognized, but some other foreign language, maybe French. He wasn't sure. He scowled after them. Who they think they are, walking around a black man's city, upnosing people like that?

He studied his reflection for a while in the burnished window of a jewelry shop. Ground floor, Martin Luther King Building. Eighty stories of polished black marble. Black. Black man's money built that tower! Black man's sweat!

Overhead came the buzz of a hopter after all. No commuters today, so they had to be tourists. James Shabazz stared up at the beetle of a hopter crossing the dull translucent background of the distant dome. It landed on the penthouse hopter stage of the King Building. He crossed the street and tried to see the palefaces stepping out, but the angle was too steep. Even so, he bowed ceremoniously. Welcome, massa! Welcome to the black man's metropolis! Soul food for lunch? Real hot jazz on 125th? Dancing jigaboo girls stripping at the Apollo? Sightseeing tour of Bedford-Stuyvesant and Harlem?

Can't tell where Bedford-Stuyvesant ends and Harlem begins, can you? But you'll come looking anyway.

Like to cut your guts up, you honkie mothers.

* * *

Martin Luther King said in Montgomery, Alabama, instructing the bus desegregators:

> *If cursed, do not curse back. If pushed, do not push back. If struck, do not strike back, but evidence love and good will at all times*

He sat down for a while in Lumumba Park, back of the 42nd Street Library, to watch the girls go by. The new summer styles were something pretty special: Congo Revival, plenty of beads and metal coils, but not much clothing except a sprayon sarong around the middle. There was a lot of grumbling by the old people. But how could you tell a handsome Afro girl that she shouldn't show her beautiful black breasts in public? Did they cover the boobies in the Motherland? Not until the missionaries came. Christ can't stand a pare of bares. The white girls cover up because they don't got much up there. Or maybe to keep from getting sunburned.

He admired the parade of proud jiggling black globes. The girls smiled to themselves as they cut through the park. They all wore their hair puffed out tribal style, and some of them even with little bone doodads thrust through it. There was no reason to be afraid of looking too primitive any more. James Shabazz winked, and some of them winked back. A few of the girls kept eyes fixed rigidly ahead; plainly it was an ordeal for them to strip down this way. Most of them enjoyed it as much as the men did. The park was full of men enjoying the show. James Shabazz wished they'd bring those honkie tourists here. He'd love a chance to operate on a few of them.

Gradually he became aware of a huge, fleshy, exceedingly black man with grizzled white hair, sitting across the way pretending to be reading his paper, but really stealing peeks at the cuties going by. James Shabazz recognized him: Powell 43X Nissim, Coordinating

Chairman of the Afro-Muslim Popular Democratic Party of Greater New York. He was one of the biggest men in the city, politically—maybe even more important than Mayor Abdulrahman himself. He was also a good friend of the father of James Shabazz, who handled some of Powell 43X's legal work. Four or five times a year he came around to discuss some delicate point, and stayed far into the night, drinking pot after pot of black coffee and telling jokes in an uproarious bellow. Most of his jokes were antiblack; he could tell them like any Kluxer. James Shabazz looked on him as coarse, vulgar, seamy, out of date, an old-line pol. But yet you had to respect a man with that much power.

Powell 43X Nissim peered over the top of his *Amsterdam News,* saw him, let out a whoop, and yelled, "Hey, Jimmy Lincoln! What you doin' here?"

James Shabazz stood up and walked stiffly over. "Getting me some fresh air, sir."

"Been working at the library, huh? Studying hard? Gonna be the first nigger president, maybe?"

"No, sir. Just walkin' around on a Saturday."

"Ought to be in the library," Powell 43X said. "Read. Learn. That's how we got where we are. You think we took over this city because we a bunch of dumb niggers?" He let out a colossal laugh. "We *smart,* man!"

James Shabazz wanted to say, "We took over the city because Whitey ran out. He dumped it on us, is all. Didn't take no brains, just staying power."

Instead he said, "I got a little time to take it easy yet, sir. I don't go to college for another year."

"Columbia, huh?"

"You bet. Class of '05, that's me."

"You gonna fool with football when you get to college?"

"Thought I would."

"You listen to me," said Powell 43X. "Football's okay for high school. You get yourself into politics instead up there. Debating team. Malcolm X Society. Afro League. Smart boy like you, you got a career in government ahead of you if you play it right." He jerked his head to one side and indicated a girl striding by. "You get to be somebody, maybe you'll have a few of those to play with." He laughed. The girl was almost six feet tall, majestic, deep black, with great heavy swinging breasts and magnificent buttocks switching saucily from side to side beneath her sprayon wrap. Conscious that all eyes were on her, she crossed the park on the diagonal, heading for the Sixth Avenue side. Suddenly three whites appeared at the park entrance: weekend visitors, edgy, conspicuous. As the black girl went past them, one turned, gaping, his eyes following the trajectory of her outthrust nipples. He was a wiry redhead, maybe twenty years old, in town for a good time in boogieville, and you could see the hunger popping out all over him.

"Honkie mother," James Shabazz muttered. "Could use a blade you know where."

Powell 43X clucked his tongue. "Easy, there. Let him look! What it hurt you if he thinks she's worth lookin' at?"

"Don't belong here. No right to look. Why can't they stay where they belong?"

"Jimmy—"

"Honkies right in Times Square! Don't they know this here's our city?"

Marcus Garvey said:

The Negro needs a Nation and a country of his own, where he can best show evidence of his own ability in the art of human progress. Scattered as an unmixed and unrecognized part of alien nations and civilizations is but to demonstrate his imbecility, and point him out as an unworthy derelict, fit neither for the society of Greek, Jew, or Gentile.

While he talked with Powell 43X, James Shabazz kept one eye on the honkie from the suburbs. The redhead and his two pales cut out in the direction of 41st Street. James Shabazz excused himself finally and drifted away, toward that side of the park. Old windbag, he thought. Nothing but a Tom underneath. Tolerance for the honkies! When did they tolerate *us?*

Easy, easy, like a panther. Walk slow and quiet.

Follow the stinking mother. Show him how it really is.

Malcolm X said:

Always bear in mind that our being in the Western hemisphere differs from anyone else, because everyone else came here voluntarily. Everyone that you see in this part of the world got on a boat and came here voluntarily; whether they were immigrants or what have you, they came here voluntarily. So they don't have any real squawk, because they got what they were looking for. But you and I can squawk because we didn't come here voluntarily. We didn't ask to be brought here. We were brought here forcibly, against our will, and in chains. And at no time since we have been here, have they even acted like they wanted us here. At no time. At no time have they ever tried to pretend that we were brought here to be citizens. Why, they don't even pretend. So why should we pretend?

The cities had been theirs for fifteen or twenty years. It had been a peaceful enough conquest. Each year there were fewer whites and more blacks, and the whites kept moving out, and the blacks kept getting born, and one day Harlem was as far south as 72nd Street, and Bedford-Stuyvesant had slopped over into Flatbush and Park Slope, and there was a black mayor and a black city council, and that was it. In New York the tipping point had come about 1986. There was a special problem there, because of the Puerto Ricans, who thought of themselves as a separate community; but they were outnumbered, and most of them finally decided it was cooler to have a city of their own. They took Yonkers, the way the Mexicans took San Diego. What it shuffled down to, in the end, was a city about eighty-five percent black and ten percent Puerto, with some isolated pockets of whites who stuck around out of stubbornness or old age or masochism or feelings of togetherness with their black brothers. Outside the city were the black suburbs like Mount Vernon and Newark and New Rochelle, and beyond them, fifty, eighty, a hundred miles out, were the towns of the whites. It was apartheid in reverse.

The honkie commuters still came into the city, those who had to, quick-in quick-out, do your work and scram. There weren't many of them, really, a hundred thousand a day or so. The white ad agencies were gone north. The white magazines had relocated editorial staffs in the green suburbs. The white book publishers had followed the financial people out. Those who came in were corporate executives, presiding over all-black staffs; trophy whites, kept around by liberal-minded blacks for decoration; government employees, trapped by desegregation edicts; and odds and ends of other sorts, all out of place, all scared.

It was a black man's city. It was pretty much the same all across the country. Adjustments had been made.

Stokely Carmichael said:

> We are oppressed as a group because we are black, not because we are lazy, not because we're apathetic, not because we're stupid, not because we smell, not because we eat watermelon and have good rhythm. We are oppressed because we are black, and in order to get out of that oppression, one must feel the group power that one has ... If there's going to be any in-

tegration it's going to be a two-way thing. If you believe in integration, you can come live in Watts. You can send your children to the ghetto schools. Let's talk about that. If you believe in integration, then we're going to start adopting us some white people to live in our neighborhood...

....We are not gonna wait for white people to sanction black power. We're tired of waiting.

South of 42nd Street things were pretty quiet on a Saturday, or any other time. Big tracts of the city were still empty. Some of the office buildings had been converted into apartment houses to catch the overflow, but a lot of them were still awaiting development. It took time for a black community to generate enough capital to run a big city, and though it was happening fast, it wasn't happening fast enough to make use of all the facilities the whites had abandoned. James Shabazz walked silently through silence, keeping his eyes on the three white boys who strolled, seemingly aimlessly, a block ahead of him.

He couldn't dig why more tourists didn't get cut up. Hardly any of them did, except those who got drunk and pawed some chick. The ones who minded their own business were left alone, because the top men had passed the word that the sightseers were okay, that they injected cash into the city and shouldn't be molested. It amazed James Shabazz that everybody listened. Up at the Audubon, somebody would get up and read from Stokely or Malcolm or one of the other black martyrs, and call for a holy war on Whitey, really socking it to 'em. Civil rights! Equality! Black power! Retribution for four hundred years of slavery! Break down the ghetto walls! Keep the faith, baby! Tell it how it is! All about the exploitation of the black man, the exclusion of the Afros from the lily-white suburbs, the concentration of economic power in Whitey's hands. And the audience would shout amen and stomp its feet and sing hymns, but nobody would ever do anything. *Nobody would ever do anything*. He couldn't understand that. Were they satisfied to live in a city with an invisible wall around it? Did they really think they had it so good? They talked about owning New York, and maybe they did, but didn't they know that it was all a fraud, that Whitey had given them the damn city just so they'd stay out of *his* back yard?

Someday we gonna run things. Not the Powell 43X cats and the other Toms, but *us*. And we gonna keep the city, but we gonna take what's outside, too.

And none of this crap about honkie mothers coming in to look our women over.

James Shabazz noted with satisfaction that the three white boys were splitting up. Two of them were going into Penn Station to grab the tube home, looked like. The third was the redhead, and he was standing by himself on Seventh Avenue, looking up at Uhuru Stadium, which he probably called Madison Square Garden. Good boy. Dumb enough to leave yourself alone. Now I gonna teach you a thing or two.

He moved forward quickly.

Robert F. Williams said:

> When an oppressed people show a willingness to defend themselves, the enemy, who is a moral weakling and coward, is more willing to grant concessions and work for a respectable compromise.

He walked up smiling and said, "Hi, man. I'm Jimmy Lincoln."

Whitey looked perplexed. "Hi, man."

"You lookin' for some fun, I bet."

"Just came in to see the city a little."

"To find some fun. Lots of great chicks around here." Jimmy Lincoln winked broadly. "You can't kid me none.

I go for 'em too. Where you from, Red?"

"Nyack."

"That's upstate somewhere, huh?"

"Not so far. Just over the bridge. Rockland County."

"Yeah. Nice up there, I bet. I never seen it."

"Not so different from down here. Buildings are smaller, that's all. Just as crowded."

"I bet they got a different-looking skin in Nyack," said Jimmy Lincoln. He laughed. "I bet I right, huh?"

The red-haired boy laughed too. "Well, I guess you are."

"Come on with me. I find you some fun. You and me. What's your name?"

"Tom."

"Tom. That's a good one. Lookee, Tom, I know a place, lots of girls, something to drink, a pill to pop, real soul music, yeah? Eh, man? Couple blocks from here. You came here to see the city, let me show it to you. Right?"

"Well—" uneasily.

"Don't be so uptight, man. You don't trust your black brother? Look, we got no feud with you. All that stuff's ancient history! You got to realize this is the year 2000, we all free men, we got what we after. Nobody gonna hurt you." Jimmy Lincoln moved closer and winked confidentially. "Lemme tell you something, too. That red hair of yours, the girls gonna orbit over that! They don't see that kind hair every day. Them freckles. Them blue eyes. Man, blue eyes, it turn them on! You in for the time of your life!"

Tom from Nyack grinned. He pointed toward Penn Station. "I came in with two pals. They went home, the geeps! Tomorrow they're going to feel awful dopey about that."

"You know they will," said Jimmy Lincoln.

They walked west, across Eighth Avenue, across Ninth, into the redevelopment area where the old warehouses

had been ripped down. Signs sprouting from the acreage
of rubble proclaimed that the Afro-American Cultural
Center would shortly rise here. Just now the area looked
bombed out. Tom from Nyack frowned as if he failed to
see where a swinging nightclub was likely to be located
in this district. Jimmy Lincoln led him up to 35th Street
and around the hollow shell of a not quite demolished
building.

"Almost there?" Tom asked.

"We here right now, man."

"Where?"

"Up against that wall, that's where," said James Shabazz. The sonic blade glided into his hand. He studded
it and it began to whirl menacingly. In a quiet voice he
said, "Honkie, I saw you look at a black girl a little while
ago like you might just be thinking about what's between
her legs. You shouldn't think thoughts like that about
black girls. You got an itch, man, you scratch it on your
own kind. I think I'm gonna fix you so you don't itch
no more."

Minister James 3X said:

*First, there is fear—first and foremost there is
inborn fear, and hatred for the black man. There is
a feeling on the part of the white man of inferiority.
He thinks within himself that the black man is the best
man.*

*The white man is justified in feeling that way be-
cause he has discovered that he is weaker than the
black man. His mental power is less than that of the
black man—he has only six ounces of brain and the
Original Man has seven-and-a-half ounces . . . The
white man's physical power is one-third less than that
of the black man.*

He had never talked this long with a honkie before. You didn't see all that many of them about, when you spent your time in high school. But now he stared into those frightened blue eyes and watched the blood drain from the scruffy white skin and he felt power welling up inside him. He was Chaka Zulu and Malcolm and Stokely and Nkrumah and Nat Turner and Lumumba all rolled into one. He, James Shabazz, was going to lead the new black revolution, and he was going to begin by sacrificing this cowering honkie. Through his mind rolled the magnificent phrases of his prophets. He heard them talking, yes, Adam and Ras Tafari and Floyd, heard them singing down the ages out of Africa, kings in chains, martyrs, the great ones, he heard Elijah Muhammad and Muhammad Ali, Marcus Garvey, Sojourner Truth, du Bois, Henry Garnet, Rap Brown, rattling the chains, shouting for freedom, and all of them telling him, go on, man, how long you want to be a nigger anyhow? Go on! You think you got it so good? You gonna go to college, get a job, live in a house, eat steak and potatoes, and that's enough, eh, nigger, even if you can't set foot in Nyack, Peekskill, Wantagh, Suffern, Morristown? Be happy with what you got, darkie! You got more than we ever did, so why bitch about things? You got a city! You got power! You got freedom! It don't matter that they call you an ape. Don't matter that they don't let you near their daughters. Don't matter that you never seen Nyack. Be grateful for what you got, man, is that the idea?

He heard their cosmic laughter, the thunder of their derision.

And he moved toward Tom the honkie and said, "Here's where the revolution gets started again. Trash like you fooling with our women, you gonna get a blade in the balls. You go home to Nyack and give 'em that message, man."

Tom said lamely, "Look out behind you!"

James Shabazz laughed and began to thrust the blade home, but the anesthetic dart caught him in the middle of the back and his muscles surrendered, and the blade fell, and he turned as he folded up and saw the black policeman with the dart gun in his black fist, and he realized that he had known all along that this was how it would turn out, and he couldn't say he really cared.

Robert Moses of SNCC was questioned in May, 1962 on the voter registration drive in Mississippi:

Q: *Mr. Moses, did you know a person named Herbert Lee?*

A: *Yes, he was a Negro farmer who lived near Liberty.*

Q: *Would you tell the Committee what Mr. Lee was doing and what happened?*

A: *He was killed on September 25th. That morning I was in McComb. The Negro doctor came by the voter registration office to tell us he had just taken a bullet out of a Negro's head. We went over to see who it was because I thought it was somebody in the voting program, and were able to identify the man as Mr. Herbert Lee, who had attended our classes and driven us around the voting area, visiting other farmers.*

Powell 43X Nissim said heavily, folding his hands across his paunch, "I got you off because you're your daddy's son. But you try a fool thing like that again, I gon' let them put you away."

James Shabazz said nothing.

"What you think you was doing, anyway, Jimmy? You know we watch all the tourists. We can't afford to let them get cut up. There was tracers on that kid all the time."

"I didn't know."

"You sit there mad as hell, thinking I should have let you cut him. You know who you really would have cut? Jimmy Lincoln, that's who. We still got jails. Black judges know the law too. You get ruined for life, a thing like that. And what for?"

"To show the honkie a thing or two."

"Jimmy, Jimmy, Jimmy! What's to show? We got the whole city!"

"Why can't we live outside?"

"Because we don't *want* to. Those of us who can afford it, even, we stay here. They got laws against discrimination in this country. We stay here because we like it with our own kind. Even the black millionaires, and don't think there ain't plenty of 'em. We got a dozen men, they could *buy* Nyack. They stay."

"And why do you stay?"

"I'm in politics," said Powell 43X. "You know what a power base means? I got to stay where my people are. I don't care about living with the whites."

"You talk like you aren't even sore about it," James Shabazz said. "Don't you hate Whitey?"

"No. I don't hate no one."

"We all hate Whitey!"

"Only you hate Whitey," said Powell 43X. "And that's because you don't know nothin' yet. The time of hating's over, Jimmy. We got to be practical. You know, we got ourselves a good deal now, and we ain't gon' get more by burning nobody. Well, maybe the Stock Exchange moved to Connecticut, and a lot of banks and stuff like that, but *we run the city*. Black men. Black men hold the mortgages. We got a black upper crust here now. Fancy shops for black folk, fancy restaurants, black banks, gorgeous mosques. Nobody oppressing us now. When a mortgage gets foreclosed these days, it a *black* man doin' the foreclosin'. Black men ownin' the sweatshops. Ownin' the hockshops. Good and bad, we got the city, Jimmy.

And maybe this is the way it meant to be: us in the cities, them outside."

"You talk like a Tom!"

"And you talk like a fool." Powell 43X chuckled. "Jimmy, wake up! We all Toms today. We don't do revolutions now."

"I go to the Audubon," James Shabazz said. "I listen to them speak. They talk revolution there. They don't sound like no Toms to me!"

"It's all politics, son. Talk big, yell for equality. It don't make sense to let a good revolution die. They do it for show. A man don't get anywhere politickin' in black New York by sayin' that everything's one hundred percent all right in the world. And you took all that noise seriously? You didn't know that they just shoutin' because it's part of the routine? You went out to spear you a honkie? I figured you for smarter than that. Look, you all mixed up, boy. A smart man, black or white, he don't mess up a good deal for himself, even if he sometimes say he *want* to change everything all around. You full of hate, full of dreams. When you grow up, you'll understand. Our problem, it's not how to get out into the suburbs, it's how to keep Whitey from wanting to come back and live in here! We got to keep what we got. We got it pretty good. Who oppressing you, Jimmy? You a slave? Wake up! And now you understand the system a little better, clear your rear end outa my office. I got to phone up the mayor and have a little talk."

Jimmy Lincoln stumbled out, stunned, shaken. His eyes felt hot and his tongue was dry. The system? The *system?* How cynical could you get? The whole revolution phony? All done for show?

No. No. No. No.

He wanted to smash down the King Building with his fists. He wanted to see buildings ablaze, as in the old days when the black man was still fighting for what ought to be his.

I don't believe it, he thought. Not any of it. I'm not gonna stop fighting for my rights. I'm gonna live to see us overcome. I won't sell out like the others. Not me!

And then he thought maybe he was being a little dumb. Maybe Powell 43X was right: there wasn't anything left worth fighting for, and only a dopey kid would take the slogans at face value. He tried to brush that thought out of his head. If Powell 43X was right, everything he had read was a lot of crap. Stokely. Malcolm. All the great martyrs. Just so much ancient history?

He stepped out into the summer haze. Overhead, a hopterbus was heading for the suburbs. He shook his fist at it; and instantly he felt foolish for the gesture, and wondered why he felt foolish. And knew. And beneath his rebellious fury, began to suspect that one day he'd give in to the system too. But not yet. Not yet!

time to do my homework now

machine, spell everything right today's essay is on black power as a revolutionary force I am James Lincoln, Class 804, Frederick Douglass High School put that heading on the page yeah

the concept of black power as a revolutionary force first was heard during the time of oppression forty years ago, when

crap on that, machine, we better hold it until I know what I going to say

I am James Shabazz age seventeen born august 13 1983 I am black I am afro I am beautiful

black is beautiful

let's start over, machine

let's make an outline first

black power its origin its development the martyrdoms and lynchings the first black mayors the black congressmen and senators the black cities and then talk about black power as a continuing thing, the never-ending revolution no matter what pols like 43X say, never give in never settle for what they give you never sell out

that's it, machine
black power
black
black is beautiful

RINGING THE CHANGES

There has been a transmission error in the shunt room, and several dozen bodies have been left without minds, while several dozen minds are held in the stasis net, unassigned and, for the moment, unassignable. Things like this have happened before, which is why changers take out identity insurance, but never has it happened to so many individuals at the same time. The shunt is postponed. Everyone must be returned to his original identity; then they will start over. Suppressing the news has proved to be impossible. The area around the hospital has been besieged by the news media. Hovercameras stare rudely at the building at every altitude from twelve to twelve hundred feet. Trucks are angle-parked in the street. Journalists trade tips, haggle with hospital personnel for the names of the bereaved, and seek to learn the identities of those involved in the mishap. "If I knew, I'd tell you," says Jaime Rodriguez, twenty-seven. "Don't you think I could use the money? But we don't know. That's the whole trouble, we don't know. The data tank was the first thing to blow."

The shunt room has two antechambers, one on the west side of the building, the other facing Broadway; one is occupied by those who believe they are related to the victims, while in the other can be found the men from the insurance companies. Like everyone else, the insurance men have no real idea of the victims' names, but they do know that various clients of theirs were due for shunting today, and with so many changers snarled up at once, the identity-insurance claims may ultimately run into the millions. The insurance men confer agitatedly with one another, dictate muttered memoranda, scream telephone calls into their cufflinks, and show other signs of distress, although several of them remain cool enough to conduct ordinary business while here; they place stock market orders and negotiate assignations with nurses. It is, however, a tense and difficult situation, whose final implications are yet unknown.

Dr. Vardaman appears, perspired, paternal. "We're making every effort," he says, "to reunite each changer with the proper identity matrix. I'm fully confident. Only a matter of time. Your loved ones, safe and sound."

"We aren't the relatives," says one of the insurance men.

"Excuse me," says Dr. Vardaman, and leaves.

The insurance men wink and tap their temples knowingly. They peer beyond the antechamber door.

"Cost us a fortune," one broker says.

"Not your money," an adjuster points out.

"Raise premiums, I guess."

"Lousy thing. Lousy thing. Lousy thing. Could have been me."

"You a changer?"

"Due for a shunt next Tuesday."

"Tough luck, man. You could have used a vacation."

The antechamber door opens. A plump woman with dark-shadowed eyes enters. "Where are they?" she asks. "I want to see them! My husband was shunting today!"

She begins to sob and then to shriek. The insurance men rush to comfort her. It will be a long and somber day.

NOW GO ON WITH THE STORY

After a long time in the stasis net, the changer decides that something must have gone wrong with the shunt. It has never taken this long before. Something as simple as a shift of persona should be accomplished quickly, like the pulling of a tooth: *out, shunt, in.* Yet minutes or possibly hours have gone by, and the shunt has not come. What are they waiting for? I paid good money for a shunt. Something wrong somewhere, I bet.

Get me out of here. Change me.

The changer has no way of communicating with the hospital personnel. The changer, at present, exists only as a pattern of electrical impulses held in the stasis net. In theory it is possible for an expert to communicate in code even across the stasis gap, lighting up nodes on a talkboard; it was in this way that preliminary research into changing was carried out. But this changer has no such skills, being merely a member of the lay public seeking temporary identity transformation, a holiday sojourn in another's skull. The changer must wait in limbo.

A voice impinges. "This is Dr. Vardaman, addressing all changers in the net. There's been a little technical difficulty, here. What we need to do now is put you all back in the bodies you started from, which is just a routine reverse shunt, as you know, and when everybody is sorted out we can begin again. Clear? So the next thing that's going to happen to you is that you'll get shunted, only you won't be changed, heh-heh, at least we don't *want* you to be changed. As soon as you're able to speak to us, please tell your nurse if you're back in the right body, so we can disconnect you from the master switchboard, all right? Here we go, now, one, two, three—"

* * *

—*shunt*.

this body is clearly the wrong one, for it is female. The changer trembles, taking possession of the cerebral fibres and driving pitons into the autonomic nervous system. A hand rises and touches a breast. Erectile tissue responds. The skin is soft and the flesh is firm. The changer strokes a cheek. Beardless. He searches now for vestigial personality traces. He finds a name, Vonda Lou, and the image of a street, wide and dusty, a small town in a flat region, with squat square-fronted buildings set well back from the pavement, and gaudy automobiles parked sparsely in front of them. Beyond the town the zone of dry red earth begins; far away are the bare brown mountains. This is no place for the restless. A soothing voice says, "They catch us, Vonda Lou, they gonna take a baseball bat, jam it you know where," and Vonda Lou replies, "They ain't gone catch us anyway," and the other voice says, "But if they do, but if they do?" The room is warm but not humid. There are crickets outside. Cars without mufflers roar by. Vonda Lou says, "Stop worrying and put your head here. *Here*. That's it. Oh, nice—" There is a giggle. They change positions. Vonda Lou says, "No fellow ever did that to you, right?" The soft voice says, "Oh, Vonda Lou—" And Vonda Lou says, "One of these days we gone get out of this dime-store town—" Her hands clutch yielding flesh. In her mind dances the image of a drum majorette parading down the dusty main street, twirling a baton, lifting knees high and pulling the white shorts tight over the smug little rump, yes, yes, look at those things jiggle up there, look all the nice stuff, and the band plays *Dixie* and the football team comes marching by, and Vonda Lou laughs, thinking of that big hulking moron and how he had tried to dirty her, putting his paws all over her, that dumb Billy Joe who figured he was going to score, and all the time Vonda Lou was laughing at him inside, because it wasn't the halfback but the drum majorette who had what she wanted, and—

Voice: "Can you hear me? If there has been a proper matching of body and mind, please raise your right hand."

The changer lifts his left hand.

—*shunt*

The world here is dark green within a fifty-yard radius of the helmet lamp, black beyond. The temperature is 38 degrees F. The pressure is six atmospheres. One moves like a crab within one's jointed suit, scuttling along the bottom. Isolated clumps of gorgonians wave in the current. To the left, one can see as though through a funnel the cone of light that rises to the surface, where the water is blue. Along the face of the submerged cliff are coral outcroppings, but not here, not this deep, where sunlight never reaches and the sea is of a primal coldness.

One moves cautiously, bothered by the pressure drag. One clutches one's collecting rod tightly, stepping over nodules of manganese and silicon, swinging the lamp in several directions, searching for the place where the bottom drops away. One is uneasy and edgy here, not because of the pressure or the dark or the chill, but because one is cursed with an imagination, and one cannot help but think of the kraken in the pit. One dreams of Tennyson's dreamless beast, below the thunders of the upper deep. Faintest sunlights flee about his shadowy sides: above him swell huge sponges of millennial growth and height.

One comes now to the brink of the abyss.

There hath he lain for ages and will lie, battening upon huge seaworms in his sleep, until the latter fire shall heat the deep; then once by man and angels to be seen, in roaring he shall rise and on the surface die. Yes. One is moved, yes. One inclines one's lamp, hoping its beam will strike a cold glittering eye below. Far, far beneath in the abysmal sea. There is no sign of the thick ropy tentacles, the mighty beak.

"Going down in, now," one says to those above.

One has humor as well as imagination. One pauses at the brink, picks up a chalky stone, inscribes on a boulder crusted with the tracks of worms the single word:

NEMO

One laughs and flips aside the stone, and launches one's self into the abyss, kicking off hard against the continental shelf. Down. And down. Seeking wondrous grot and secret cell.

The changer sighs, thinking of debentures floated on the Zurich exchange, of contracts for future delivery of helium and plutonium, of puts and calls and margins. He will not enter the abyss; he will not see the kraken; feebly he signals with his left hand.

—shunt

A middle-aged male, at least. There's hope in that. A distinct paunch at the middle. Some shortness of breath. Faint stubble on face. The legs feel heavy with swollen feet; a man gets tired easily at a certain age, when his responsibilities are heavy. The sound of unanswered telephones rings in his ears. Everything is familiar: the tensions, the frustrations, the fatigue, the sense of things unfinished and things uncommenced, the staleness in the mouth, the emptiness in the gut. This must be the one. Home again, all too soon?

Q: Sir, in the event of an escalation of the crisis, would you request an immediate meeting of the Security Council, or would you attempt to settle matters through quasi-diplomatic means as was done in the case of the dispute between Syria and the Maldive Islands?

A: Let's not put the horse in the cart, shall we?

Q: According to last Monday's statement by the Bureau of the Budget, this year's deficit is already running twelve billion ahead of last, and we're only halfway through the second quarter. Have you given any concern to the accusation of the Fiscal Responsibility Party that this is the result of a deliberate Communist-dictated plan to demoralize the economy?

A: What do you think?

Q: Is there any thought of raising the tax on personality-shunting?

A: Well, now, there's already a pretty steep tax on that, and we don't want to do anything that'll interfere with the rights of American citizens to move around from body to body, as is their God-given and constitutional right. So I don't think we'll change that tax any.

Q: Sir, we understand that you yourself have done some shunting. We—

A: Where'd you hear that?

Q: I think it was Representative Spear, of Iowa, who said the other day that it's well known that the President visits a shunt room every time he's in New York, and—

A: You know these Republicans. They'll say anything at all about a Democrat.

Q: Mr. President, does the Administration have any plans for ending sexual discrimination in public washrooms?

A: I've asked the Secretary of the Interior to look into that, inasmuch as it might involve interstate commerce and also being on Federal property, and we expect a report at a later date.

Q: Thank you, Mr. President.

The left hand stirs and rises. Not this one, obviously.
The hand requests a new phase-shift. The body is properly soggy and decayed, yes. But one must not be deceived by superficialities. This is the wrong one. Out,
please. Out.

—shunt

The crowd stirred in anticipation as Bernie Kingston
left the on-deck circle and moved toward the plate, and
by the time he was in the batter's box they were standing.

Kingston glanced out at the imposing figure of Ham
Fillmore, the lanky Hawks southpaw on the mound. *Go
ahead,* Bernie thought. *I'm ready for you.*

He wiggled the bat back and forth two or three times
and dug in hard, waiting for the pitch. It was a low, hard
fastball, delivered by way of first base, and it shot past
him before he had a chance to offer. "Strike one," he
heard. He looked down toward third to see if the manager
had any sign for him.

But Danner was staring at him blankly. *You're on your
own,* he seemed to be saying.

The next pitch was right in the groove, and Bernie
lined it effortlessly past the big hurler's nose and on into
right field for a single. The crowd roared its approval as
he trotted down to first.

"Good going, kid," said Jake Edwards, the first-base
coach, when Bernie got there. Bernie grinned. Base hits
always felt good, and he loved to hear the crowd yell.

The Hawks' catcher came out to the mound and called
a conference. Bernie wandered around first, doing some
gardening with his spikes. With one out and the score
tied in the eighth, he couldn't blame the Hawks for wanting to play it close to the belt.

As soon as the mound conference broke up it was the
Stags' turn to call time. "Come here, kid," Jake Edwards
called.

"What's the big strategy this time?" Bernie asked boredly.

"No lip, kid. Just go down on the second pitch."

Bernie shrugged and edged a few feet off the base. Ham Fillmore was still staring down at his catcher, shaking off signs, and Karl Folsom, the Stag cleanup man, was waiting impatiently at the plate.

"Take a lead," the coach whispered harshly. "Go on, Kingston—get down that line."

The hurler finally was satisfied with his sign, and he swung into the windup. The pitch was a curve, breaking far outside. Folsom didn't venture at it, and the ball hit the dirt and squirted through the catcher's big mitt. It trickled about fifteen feet back of the plate.

Immediately the Hawks' shortstop moved in to cover second in case Bernie might be going. But Bernie had no such ideas. He stayed put at first.

"What's the matter, lead in ya pants?" called a derisive voice from the Hawk dugout.

Bernie snarled something and returned to the base. He glanced over at third, and saw Danner flash the steal sign.

He leaned away from first cautiously, five, six steps, keeping an eye cocked at the mound.

The pitcher swung into a half-windup—Bernie broke for second—his spikes dug furiously into the dusty basepath—

Out! Out! Out! The left hand upraised! Not this one, either! Out! Get me out!

—shunt!

Through this mind go dreams of dollars, and the changer believes they have finally made the right matchup. He takes the surroundings and finds much here that is familiar. Dow-Jones Industrials 1453.28, down 8.29. Confirmation of the bear signal by the rails. Penetration of the August 13 lows. Watch the arbitrage spread you get by going short on the common while picking up 10,000 of the $1.50 convertible preferred at—

The substance is right; so is the context. But the tone is wrong, the changer realizes. This man loves his work.

The changer tours this man's mind from the visitors' gallery.

—we can unload 800 shares in Milan at 48, which gives us two and a half points right there, and then after they announce the change in redemption ratio I think we ought to drop another thousand on the Zurich board—

—give me those Tokyo quotes! Damn you, you sleepy bastard, don't slow me up! Here, here, Kansai Electric Power, I want the price in yen, not the American Depository crap—

—pick up twenty-two per cent of the voting shares through street names before we announce the tender offer, that's the right way to do it, then hit them hard from a position of strength and watch the board of directors fold up in two days—

—I think we can work it with the participating preference stock, if we give them just a little hint that the dividend might go up in January, and of course they don't have to know that after the merger we're going to throw them all out anyway, so—

—why am I in it? Why, for the fun of it!—

Yes. The sheer joy of wielding power. The changer lingers here, sadly wondering why it is that this man, who after all functions in the same environment as the changer himself, shows such fierce gusto, such delight in finance for the sake of finance, while the changer derives only sour tastes and dull aches from all his getting. It's because he's so young, the changer decides. The thrill hasn't yet worn off for him. The changer surveys the body in which he is temporarily a resident. He makes himself aware of the flat belly's firm musculature, of the even rhythms of the heart, of the lean flanks. This man is at most forty years old, the changer concludes. Give him thirty more years and ten million dollars and he'll know how hollow it all is. The futility of existence, the changer thinks. You feel it at seventeen, you feel it at seventy, but often you fail to feel it in between. I feel it. I feel it. And so this body can't be mine. Lift the left hand. Out.

"We are having some difficulties," Dr. Vardaman confesses, "in achieving accurate pairings of bodies and minds." He tells this to the insurance men, for there is every reason to be frank with them. "At the time of transmission error we were left with—ah—twenty-nine minds in the stasis net. So far we've returned eleven of them to their proper bodies. The others—"

"Where are the eleven?" asks an adjuster.

"They're recuperating in the isolation ward," Dr. Vardaman replies. "You understand, they've been through three or four shunts apiece today, and that's pretty strenuous. After they've rested, we'll offer them the option to undergo the contracted-for change as scheduled, or to take a full refund."

"Meanwhile we got eighteen possible identity-insurance claims," says another of the insurance men. "That's something like fifteen million bucks. We got to know what you're doing to get the others back in the right bodies."

"Our efforts are continuing. It's merely a matter of time until everyone is properly matched."

"And if some of them die while you're shunting them?"

"What can I say?" Dr. Vardaman says. "We're making every attempt."

To the relatives he says, "There's absolutely no cause for alarm. Another two hours and we'll have it all straightened out. Please be assured that none of the clients involved are suffering any hardship or inconvenience, and in fact this may be a highly interesting and entertaining experience for them."

"My husband," the plump woman says. "Where's my husband?"

—shunt

The changer is growing weary of this. They have had him in five bodies, now. How many more times will they shove him about? Ten? Twenty? Sixteen thousand? He knows that he can free himself from this wheel of transformations at any time. Merely raise the right hand, claim a body as one's own. They'd never know. Walk right out of the hospital, threatening to sue everybody in sight; they scare easily and won't interfere. Pick your body. Be anyone who appeals to you. Pick fast, though, because if you wait too long they'll hit the right combination and twitch you back into the body you started from. Tired, defeated, old, do you want that?

Here's your chance, changer. Steal another man's body. Another woman's if that's your kick. You could have walked out of here as that dyke from Texas. Or that diver. That ballplayer. That hard young market sharpie. Or the President. Or this new one, now—take your pick, changer.

What do you want to be? Essence precedes existence. They offer you your choice of bodies. Why go back to your own? Why pick up a stale identity, full of old griefs?

The changer considers the morality of such a deed.

The chances are good of getting away with it. Others in this mess are probably doing the same thing; it's musical chairs with souls, and if eight or nine take the wrong bodies, they'll never get it untangled. Of course, if I switch, someone else switches and gets stuck with my body. Aging. Decrepit. Who wants to be a used-up stockbroker? On the other hand, the changer realizes, there are consolations. The body he wishes to abandon is wealthy, and that wealth would go to the body's claimant. Maybe someone thought of that already, and grabbed my identity. Maybe that's why I'm being shunted so often into these others. The shunt-room people can't find the right one.

The changer asks himself what his desires are.

To be young again? To play Faust? No. Not really. He wants to rest. He wants peace. There is no peace for him in returning to his proper self. Too many ghosts await him there. The changer's needs are special.

The changer examines this latest body into which he has been shunted.

Quite young. Male. Undergraduate, mind stuffed full of Kant, Hegel, Fichte, Kierkegaard. Wealthy family. Curling red hair; sleek limbs; thoughts of willing girls, holidays in Hawaii, final exams, next fall's clothing styles. Adonis on a lark, getting himself changed as a respite from the academic pace? But no: the changer probes more deeply and finds a flaw, a fatal one. There is anguish beneath the young man's self-satisfaction, and rightly so, for this body is defective, it is gravely marred. The changer is surprised and saddened, and then feels joy and relief, for this body fills his very need and more. He sees for himself the hope of peace with honor, a speedier exit, a good deed. It is a far, far better thing. He will volunteer.

His right hand rises. His eyes open.

"This is the one," he announces. "I'm home again!" His conscience is clear.

Once the young man was restored to his body, the doctors asked him if he still wished to undergo the change he had contracted for. He was entitled to this one final adventure, which they all knew would have to be his last changing, since the destruction of the young man's white corpuscles was nearly complete. No, he said, he had had enough excitement during the mixup in the shunt room, and craved no further changes. His doctors agreed he was wise, for his body might not be able to stand the strain of another shunt; and they took him back to the terminal ward. Death came two weeks later, peacefully, very peacefully.

TRANSLATION ERROR

Several strange objects were glittering in the amber depths of his detector plate, and Karn felt a gnawing uneasiness. It was only a few minutes after the ship's conversion out of the null-continuum onto the world-line of Earth, after the long nullspace voyage from Karn's distant home world.

Absent-mindedly Karn let his body cells flow into the Earther shape he had worn on his last visit, almost fifty years earlier, while he brooded over the rapidly moving objects in the detector plate. They seemed to be small bodies locked in orbit round the blue-green world below. They made no sense at all. The obvious explanation was that they were artificial planetary satellites, but surely that was impossible! Nine tiny metal moons, each in its own elliptical orbit—the implications of that made Karn feel sick. Earth could *not* have reached this stage along the technological scale yet, he told himself flatly. His computations could not have erred.

Or could they have?

Karn felt a chill invading his limbs. He went about the routine business of setting up his one-man ship for

a landing and tried to forget the annoying existence of
those nine artificial satellites. Rapidly he converted to
planetary drive, switching off the nullspace translator that
had brought him along the megaparsec-wide gulf between
his home world and Earth, and headed into the descend-
ing series of spiralling orbits that would land him.

Artificial satellites, he thought dismally. *How could
such a thing be?*

Karn checked the flow of despair that threatened to
overwhelm him. What had been done could be undone
again; if Earth somehow had reached the threshold of
space despite all his careful work in 1916, he would
simply have to take steps to correct that trend. He wondered who it was that had put the satellites up. The
Germans, obviously. Scientifically and politically, they
would be dominating the Earth in the year—what was
it?—1959.

Yes, it had to be the Germans. America had the tech-
nologically inclined minds, but America, slumbering behind its 180 years of isolation, would hardly have any
interest in conquering space. The Americans hardly knew
there were other nations on their own world, let alone
whole other worlds.

And no other nation seemed likely candidates for ownership of the accursed satellites. Certainly not France or
Britain, crushed under the Kaiser's heel in 1916. Nor old
medieval Russia, comfortably vegetating beneath the Czar.
Italy? Austria–Hungary?

Possibly Japan, he thought. The Japanese might have
put the things up.

But, Karn realized drearily, neither Germany nor Japan had as much as developed efficient airpower in 1916;
it was incredible that in a bare forty-odd years they could
have hurled orbiting satellites into space. Such a technological advance could have been stimulated only by
war.

And, thought Karn, unless his computations were

wrong for the first time in centuries, there had been no war on Earth since 1916, since the Treaty of Düsseldorf. He had carefully arranged things the last time. By keeping America out of the war, he had ensured German triumph, German dominion over all western Europe. His computations had predicted at least seventy years of peace before the broken revolutionary movement in Russia at last recovered its strength, hurled the Czar from his throne, and challenged Germany's dominance. On his last visit he had removed the stimulus of immediate war. Yet space satellites circled the Earth.

Something had gone wrong, Karn thought bleakly. But given time he could put things to rights again.

His ship sliced down into the upper layers of the atmosphere. To his surprise, he discovered that the radio-activity of Earth's atmosphere had increased remarkably in the last forty years. Did that mean that the Earthers had unleashed nuclear energy *too*?

Something was very wrong. Karn feared he had plenty of work on his hands.

His original plans had called for him to make a landing in America, and for the moment he did not intend to alter those plans. He made the landing under cover of scramblers; forty years ago such pains had been unnecessary, but who knew now what sort of technology these Earthers had developed? For all he knew they had developed a dectector system, too. It would be ignominious for him to be blasted out of the sky as a possible attacker. And until he had found out what the state of things was on Earth, it was madness to take risks. He landed under scramblers, totally impervious to detection. A neutrino-dectector might have spotted him successfully—but, thought Karn, if they had invented neutrino-detectors, too, he might just as well turn around and go back to Hethivar with the doleful news that Terran invaders would be on their way sooner than they had dreamed. The neutrino screen came *much* later in the planet's development. Normal races didn't go from animal-drawn buggies to neutrino screens in fifty years, Karn thought.

Normal races didn't go from buggies to atomics and orbital satellites in fifty years either, Karn reflected. But who said these Earthers were normal?

He landed the ship in a pleasantly green meadow in the state across the river from New York. He could remember New York, all right, but the other state's name eluded him for the moment. New Guernsey? New Calais? Ah! *New Jersey.* That was it. He left the ship parked in New Jersey, having first keyed in the external scrambler that rotated the ship one-quarter turn out of the worldline. It wavered and vanished. No one would find it where it was now, though Karn could restore it to the continuum with a minimal outlay of energy, whenever he pleased.

His first step was to transport himself autokinetically across the river into New York City. The city had grown somewhat since 1916, but he had expected that. His extrapolation had foretold a building boom trending towards giantism. It was relieving to find one aspect of Earth following expectation.

The Hethivarian hovered invisibly over a Manhattan street long enough to pick out a likely entity for duplication. He would need a working identity while he was here.

He chose a man almost at random from a group of identically clad humans in grey suits and entered his mind long enough to duplicate the information he needed. Withdrawing, Karn made the necessary transformation and allowed himself to materialize.

Now he wore contemporary American clothes and the contemporary close-cropped hair style. In the trouser pocket of his flannel suit was a wallet duplicating in every respect that of the unsuspecting individual walking ahead. Karn had an ample supply of currency now—the paper money was smaller in size than it had been, Karn noted—as well as the necessary documents for survival and a ready-made familiarity with current events and contemporary slang.

He had no desire to encroach on the identity of the man he had momentarily entered, and so as he walked along he made minor alterations in the body he wore, thickening the ears, adding a moustache, deepening the facial lines. He increased the body weight by about a fifth. No one would mistake him for the other now.

All right, he thought. He could bluff the rest of the way. *Now to catch up on news events since 1916, and see just how I could have been so wrong.*

Karn already had a picture of the way Earth *should* have looked. He had spent several years on the planet in the past, rushing there in 1914 at the outbreak of war and rapidly healing the breaches until peace became possible two years later.

From his own extrapolations and from the computed results, he had expected the German Empire to be the world's dominant state, fat with its network of global colonies, replete with conquest and sanely satiated. Germany had all the territory it wanted or needed; it would embark on no campaign of world conquest. The status would remain quo. America, having been kept out of the Great War by Karn's careful intervention, would have clasped the Monroe Doctrine to itself even more firmly and would have shut itself away from the troublesome world out across the oceans. Russia would be drowsing under the yoke of the Czar. Peace would pervade the Earth.

A pleasant peace, an era of good feelings.

Karn's motive was simple. The first scouts visiting Earth, more than a century before, had reported a vigorous and appallingly inventive race, just entering its mechanical age. The computed extrapolations had given the Hethivarian Network its biggest jolt in a millennium. They showed that Earth would be twice convulsed by war in the next century, each time taking a giant stride up the technological ladder. Without external meddling, the Earthers would leap right into the space age with frightening speed. Probabilities showed a 32 per cent chance that the quarrelsome Earthers would destroy themselves in a hundred years—and a 68 per cent chance that they would not, but instead would channel their dynamic forces and leap outward.

Extrapolations indicated that in a mere five centuries the Earthers would be, unless they managed to destroy themselves meanwhile, colonizing the stars—challenging the might of the age-old Hethivarian Network itself!

It was a frightening thought, indeed. In five centuries the Earthers would accomplish what it had taken Hethivar untold millenniums to do. They had to be stopped, for the sake of the galactic balance.

A little study showed that there were two ways to stop the Earthmen—and since one, the immediate obliteration of Earth by ultrabomb, was utterly repugnant to the highly civilized Hethivarians, there actually was only one way open. Internal intervention was called for. A trained Hethivarian agent would have to go to Earth and ease the pressures, turn down the steam under the kettle, pull back on the reins.

All that needed to be done was to remove the stimulus of war, which led to technological upspurts. A placid and untroubled Earth might sink into an amiably slothful way of life; the fierce spark that burned there might die down. So Karn was sent, and Karn engineered a peace. Not a lasting peace, of course—Earth would not be ready for that for a long time—but a stopgap, good for sixty or seventy years. When the next crisis arrived, it could be dealt with the same way. And the next, and the next, and the next—and so on into the distant future, if necessary. It was a sound plan. It would keep the Earthers from barking at the gates of the Network for centuries. It would maintain the calm balance of peace that had existed in the universe for so many thousands of years.

But, thought Karn, something had slipped up.

He would have to find a library and check up on recent history. First, though, he decided to purchase a newspaper. Entering his borrowed memory, he learned that newspapers could be bought with small silver coins. They were sold along the streets.

Karn pulled change from his pocket, selected a dime, and bought a *Times*. He scanned the front page rapidly.

Cold terror rippled through him.

Monstrous! he thought in baffled shock.

The headlines screamed incomprehensible things at him:

> PRESIDENT CALLS FOR INCREASE IN FOREIGN AID
> RUSSIA TURNS DOWN NEW PARLEY OFFER
> SATELLITE LAUNCHING POSTPONED ONE WEEK
> H-BOMB TEST A SUCCESS, WHITE HOUSE SAYS
> GERMANS COOL TO REUNIFICATION HINTS

After the first instant of disorientation was over, Karn made the necessary adjustments in his metabolism to calm himself. The newspaper was a journal of a world of nightmares. He found himself near a small park breaking up the busy streets, and on uncertain legs he made his way to a bench and sat heavily down.

Next to him a stubblefaced man said, "You look sick, buddy. Everything okay?"

Karn had enough control of himself to find the right words. "My horse didn't make it, that's all. Stay away from sure things."

"A-men, pal!"

Karn smiled to himself. It was good to know he could handle a Terran colloquial conversation so skillfully. But the smile vanished as he returned his attention to the newspaper. He read it carefully and in detail, memorizing blocks of information as he went, and within fifteen

minutes he had read his way through from end to end
and could begin shaping the scattered data into a pattern.

Everything had gone completely haywire.

Germany was a fifth-rate country now, not the king-
pin. Apparently there had been some sort of second Great
War in the past few decades; Germany had been beaten
and now lay helplessly divided. The powers on Earth
today were the United States and Russia, glaring at each
other menacingly in an uneasy stalemate.

Technological development had been catastrophically
rapid. The infernal creatures had not only developed fis-
sion weapons but fusion ones as well, and evidently
fission-fusion-fission bombs to boot. Work was progress-
ing on control of thermonuclear energy.

And, spurred on by the threat of atomic war, a vast
missile program was under way, and almost as a by-
product of the arms race, space was being conquered.
The unbelievable Earthers had hoisted more than a dozen
satellites into orbit, and work was advancing on the problem of reaching the Moon by rocket.

Karn's mind automatically supplied the gloomy extrapolation. The Moon in ten years or less, the other
planets by the end of the century, then a lull while a
nullspace drive is invented, and then the conquest of the
stars. Exactly as the first scouts had foreseen a century
ago, only faster. How could this be possible? All his
work of 1914–16 had gone completely to waste. If anything, things were worse than they would have been if
he hadn't meddled.

None of it made any sense.

Karn knew what he had to do now. First, find a library
and discover how this state of affairs had come about.
Second, contact Hethivar by subradio and report on the
situation. If ever there were a case for passing the buck,
this was it. Something had to be done, and fast. But Karn
was in no mood for making top-level decisions. Right

now it was all he could do to cling to his sanity in the face of what had happened.

He found the nearest library and located a bulky world history, and scanned it rapidly, beginning in the midnineteenth century and working forward. When he was finished, he was as close to sheer panic as he had ever been in his long life. It was an effort simply to hang on to his physical manifestation and keep from wavering. It was necessary for him to go through all nine of the Stabilizing Exercises, one after another—a humiliating experience for one who had always prided himself on his coolness.

But yet what he had discovered could easily have destabilized a lesser man.

Terran history ran precisely as it should have run, right up to 1914. In the latter half of the nineteenth century, the pressures of industrialization and the stresses of upsurging nationalism had built up conflicts certain to erupt into war. That was as expected. In 1914, the war had broken out. That, too, was acceptable. The Hethivarian Planners had decided to permit the war to begin, as a sort of catharsis for the Earthmen, but to end the war before any serious changes in the Terran way of life could be brought about.

Yet the war had *not* ended at Düsseldorf in 1916, Karn discovered. Maddeningly, there was no mention of the Allied surrender nor of the Treaty of Düsseldorf. Instead, the Germans had gone ahead and provoked America into entering the war in 1917; almost simultaneously, the Russian revolutionists had successfully overthrown the Czar. It was an unbelievable jolt to read of Germany's defeat, then of the foolish and suicidal peace settlement of 1919.

Defeated Germany had rebuilt its strength, with a madman named Hitler feeding on wounded national pride. And Russia had blindingly leaped into the twentieth century, shedding its medieval past and becoming an important world power overnight. Then, a second war,

America drawn once again—and this time permanently—from its isolationist shell, Germany and its new ally Japan decisively crushed, Russia advancing to dominate half the world, atomic weapons actually used in battle—

Nightmare, Karn thought.

He searched through rows of books, hoping to find but one mention of the Treaty of Düsseldorf, his masterpiece, which had brought all Terran friction to a halt. Not one index had an entry of that sort. Panic assailed him. His grip on the universe tottered.

It was as if he had never come to Earth to end the Great War. Not one of his interventions had as much as survived in the pages of history. And matters stood at a dreadful impasse right now. The Earthers had already conquered space—twenty years ahead of the original extrapolation, a century or more ahead of Karn's revised estimate.

Earth hovered on the brink of self-destruction. That would be too bad for Earth, Karn thought. But—far worse for the galaxy as a whole—Earth also hovered at the edge of its space age. Nightmare of nightmares!

Hethivar had to be told of this. Immediately, before Karn could make another move. Hethivar had to know.

It was a simple matter to enter a washroom on the third floor of the library building and depart autokinetically for the New Jersey meadow. No one had seen him enter the washroom, and so no one would be perturbed by his failure to come out.

Arriving at the meadow with virtual instantaneity, Karn activated the scrambler key long enough for him to enter his ship, then once again returned to concealment. Switching on the subspace communicator, he framed a message to the Hethivarian Planners:

Esteemed Sirs—

The report of Karn 1832j4, assigned to Terran Manipulation. Good sirs, matters here have reached an unaccountable state. Manipulation activity of the previous visit has been totally negated. The Earthers have fought a second war and now have developed atomic weapons and orbital satellites.

Our worst fears have come to pass. Unless immediate action is taken the Earthers will be knocking at our gates within a century.

I am unable to explain the failure of the previous mission. Obviously we must restudy our entire science of probability. But one conclusion is certain: no amount of manipulation can halt the trends already set in motion. Our only course now is a drastic one. If we are to prevent the Earthers from entering space, we may no longer strive to check war on Earth, but rather now we must foment it.

It would be a simple matter of elementary tactics for me to instigate an atomic war on Earth, considering the uneasy international condition here. Such a war would probably not result in total destruction of Terran life, but would certainly set them back many hundreds of years. Of course, this drastic step contravenes our general ethical pattern, and so I dare not take action of this sort without your permission. Yet, good sirs, surely you will see that the destiny of the galaxy is at stake here. I will await your word.

He added his wavelength, so they would be able to reach him with a reply, and signed off.

There, he thought. *That should make them sweat a little!*

Subspace communication was not quite instantaneous. There would be a lag of several minutes before the Planners received his message, and it might be hours before they had decided on their reply. Well, a few hours were not likely to make much difference. He sat back to wait.

Touching off the atomic war would be child's play, he thought. All it took was a spark in the tinder—an atomic explosion obliterating some large American or Russian city, preferably both. Within minutes, jittery defense bases would send the missiles flying. Karn's nature was such that he found the idea of such a war repugnant. But yet, if it were necessary—

He still could not understand how his calculations had gone so far astray. Bitterly he saw that it had been a mistake to allow Earth fifty years of nonintervention; there should have been a Hethivarian agent here every moment of the time. Instead Hethivar had complacently relied on its extrapolations. As he looked back, it seemed an enormously shortsighted way of handling the situation. But they had been so *confident*. Well, second sight never helped anyone, Karn thought. The only path left was the barbarous but mandatory one of smashing Earth, or rather causing Earth to smash itself.

But—

His reflections were cut off by the whirring sound of the subradio printer. A message coming back so soon? Why, they had barely had time to consider! Obviously they had met at once and voted him carte blanche.

The message said:

Karn, you blasted idiot—

Are you out of your head? Your message makes no sense at all. Your job is to avoid that atomic war, not to touch it off. And what's this jabber about preventing the Earthers from entering space? Why should we do that? And why did you change your wavelength?

Since you seem to have taken leave of your senses, you are to return to Hethivar at once. A replacement will be sent out. And if you meddle destructively in

Terran affairs you'll get immediate personality disruption when we catch you.

If this is your idea of a joke, be advised that we aren't amused. You'd better have a good explanation when you get back here.

Adric
For the Planners

Bewildered, Karn let the message slip through numb fingers. He fought to restabilize himself, and had to run through the nine Stabilizing Exercises twice. This jolt, coming on top of the earlier one, left him reeling. Had the whole universe gone mad? He was dumbfounded by Adric's message. What was he talking about? What did he mean?

Karn pondered a return message. He had gotten no further than *Highly Esteemed Sirs* when his mind unmistakably detected Hethivarian life-impressions somewhere on the planet.

His outlines blurred in dazed puzzlement. No other Hethivarian was supposed to be within a parsec of Earth at this time. True, Adric had said something about a replacement being shipped out—but it took many weeks to make the trip from Hethivar to Earth. Who could the stranger be? Cautiously, Karn extended a tendril of perception—

—encountered another mind, a Hethivarian mind—

—touched—

—recoiled in shock.

The stranger was himself!

There had been no doubt about it. Their minds had met for only a microsecond, but yet Karn had learned that the other was one Karn 1832j4, newly arrived on Earth to engage in manipulation. He had touched the surface of that other mind, and its thought-forms were his thought-forms.

Karn gripped the walls of his ship and waited for the

universe to stop spinning around him. This was what insanity was like, he thought.

A quiet voice said, "Would you mind telling me just who the devil you are?"

Karn realized the other being had come to him: He smiled and said, "You're a hallucination. Go away."

"I'm Karn. And so are you, it seems."

The other wore the body of an Earther, somewhat older, paunchy, balding. But as Karn watched, the Earther's visage gave way, in an instantaneous transition, to Karn's own. It was not like looking in the mirror, for the mirror reverses an image. This was the actual face of Karn, unfamiliar to him since he had never looked upon it in this fashion.

"We can't both be Karn," Karn said hoarsely.

"Have a look," the stranger replied, and extended his mind once again. Karn was reluctant to blend a second time; he attempted a barrier, but he was too late, and their minds joined. Karn looked deep. He saw his own thoughts laid out as neatly as he kept them, all his own memories of Hethivar. Yes, the other was himself.

But yet not himself. For mingled with the familiar memories were a host of unfamiliar ones. The other had arrived on Earth only minutes before, it seemed. But this was his third or fourth visit. He came to Earth regularly; his job was to protect the planet, to keep it from doing real harm to itself, to guide Earth along into space and into brotherhood with Hethivar.

It was like looking into a distorting mirror.

"You're here to aid Earth," Karn said.

"Yes. And you to destroy it. Destroy or else cripple. To keep the Earthers bottled up on their own world, where they can't harm the Network."

"And you're me," Karn said. "And I'm you. But we're opposite."

"Curious, isn't it? And what's this Treaty of Düsseldorf that stands out so in your mind?"

Karn said, "I arranged it, in 1916. It was supposed to provide Earth with long-lasting peace."

"To turn the Earthers into a bunch of sleepy vegetables, you mean. To rob them of the inner conflicts that would drive them into space eventually."

"And you *want* Earth to spread into space?"

"Of course," the other Karn said. "That's been our policy ever since our scouts saw the Earthers' potential. They're potentially the finest thing the universe has ever produced—but they have flaws. So we help them overcome their flaws. You think the Hethivarian Network is going to last forever?"

"No, but—"

"So why fight the inevitable? We recognize that the Earthers are potentially the next rulers of the galaxy. Okay. We take it gracefully and bow out. We don't attempt the hopeless job of trying to hold them down forever, nor do we destroy them now while we think we can. I'm here to simmer down some of their energy— to keep them from blowing themselves up, but to make sure that they rechannel those boiling drives of theirs *outward*, toward space. They're heading that way now. The Planners sent me here to make sure they get there."

Karn had never heard such a recital of insanity before in his life. But he saw clearly what had happened now. He knew why none of the history books mentioned the Treaty of Düsseldorf.

"I'm in trouble," he said.

"I'll bet you are!"

"Somehow I shifted out of my own world-line when leaving nullspace. I don't belong here at all."

Brusquely Karn made his way past the other to the control chamber. Sitting down at the control panel, he ran off a quick recheck of all the facts that had governed his conversion from the null-continuum onto Earth's worldline. It took only a few moments to find the discrepancy. He looked up at the other, his heart leaden.

"Find your mistake?" the other asked.

Karn's facial tendrils quivered in self-annoyance and shame. "Yes. I made a translation error of nearly one per cent. I came out along the wrong world-line. This isn't my universe."

"Of course not."

"And that explains why everything seemed so wrong here. The Earth *I* knew would never have sent up space satellites, nor discovered atomics. The Earth I knew would be a peaceful world."

"A vegetating world," the other snapped scornfully.

Karn scowled at him. "A world that poses no threat to the Hethivarian Network, at any rate. I'm glad this isn't *my* world-line. I'd hate to be alive when the Earthmen come swarming over our world and make us slaves. And you'll have no one to thank but yourselves."

"We'll take the risk," the other Karn rejoined sourly. "But what do *you* plan to do now?"

"Get out of this insane world-line and back to my own, as fast as I can. I have important work to do."

"Suppressing Earth's culture?"

"Insuring Hethivar's future," Karn said thinly. He went on, "I sent a message back to the Planners a little while ago. They thought it came from you, and since it didn't make any sense they ordered my recall—your recall, that is. You'd better get in touch with them and tell them what happened."

"I'll do that. Will you need any help in departing from Earth?"

Karn's eye-slits narrowed contemptuously. "I'm capable of getting back to my own world-line, thanks. It's not that hard to retrace my steps. And then I can continue my work."

"Continuing the job of bottling Earth up?"

"In my world-line," Karn said with a trace of impatience, "the preservation of Hethivar is more important to us than the coddling of Earthers. Go ahead and be altrustic—or asinine; same thing. Luckily, my world-line doesn't have to face the consequences of your actions." He chuckled. "In fact, strictly speaking, you don't even exist."

The other said testily, "May I remind you that at the moment we're both in *my* world-line—and therefore you're the nonexistent one?"

"I'll grant the point," Karn said reluctantly. "But soon I'll be back in my own continuum—the one in which I negotiated the Treaty of Düsseldorf. The one in which the Hethivarian Network will endure for eternity to come, untroubled by Earthers."

"I wish you luck," the other said dryly, and was gone.

What had happened to Karn was humiliating and annoying, but not irremediable. He had been guilty of hasty calculating, that was all; nullspace has infinite exits, and he had chosen the exit adjoining his own. Exploring probability-worlds was something Karn preferred to leave to philosophers, poets, and other dreamers; he stuck to solid reality, the one *real* world-line. All the others were mere phantoms—including, he thought in relief, the one he had just left. Earth satellites and atomics indeed! Nightmare!

He blasted off from the New Jersey meadow immediately, and, carrying each calculation out to a dozen places this time, retraced his steps, returning the ship to orbit, then converting to nullspace, finally retranslating back into what he hoped was his own world-line. He had done the routine arithmetic with scrupulous care this time. He had small fear of a second error.

He thought about the *other* Earth, the *other* Karn, as he expertly guided his ship toward Earth a second time. Karn was no narrow fool; he could understand altruism—but not suicidal altruism. It was incredible to hear someone with his own name and identity declaring solemnly and with a straight face that the proper thing to do was to *help* Earth attain space.

It was fantastic. But, Karn thought, that was what made probability-worlds, after all. Now, in *this* world-line, in the *real* universe—

He brought the ship down toward Earth and was relieved to see no orbital satellites whirling round the planet. And his radiation detectors picked up no evidence of nuclear explosions; the particle count was comfortably normal for a world that had not yet learned to harness the power of the atom—for a world that never would learn to harness it.

Karn felt warm relief. This was the world of the Treaty of Düsseldorf, at least.

Calmly and confidently, he guided the ship through the upper atmospheric levels, down toward the same pleasantly green New Jersey meadow he had used for a landing area in that other world, the world he now wanted to forget. He landed under scramblers once again; there was quite possibly no need for them, but Karn had always been cautious and now was doubly so.

He noted the time of landing in his records and prepared to leave the ship. Suddenly he sensed another intelligence nearby. For a wild instant he thought it was another Hethivarian, that he had blundered once again and landed in yet another world-line than his own. But he calmed himself and realized that this was definitely alien, definitely an Earther—

Entering the ship that was supposed to be undetectable by any method save neutrino-detector.

The Earther took form to Karn's left, against the inner wall of the ship. He was of medium height, stocky, with untidy reddish hair and coarse features. Shocked, Karn was caught midway between his own physical form and the Earthbody he adopted when dealing with the Earther.

The Hethivarian completed the change numbly, aghast at the presence of the Earther inside his ship.

"You didn't need to change shapes," the Earther said mildly. "I can see you perfectly well as you really are. Short and squat, with wavy tendrils on your face, and that big eye in the middle of your skull—"

"How did you get in here?" Karn whispered hoarsely.

"Through the wall, of course. Haven't you ever heard of intermolecular penetration? It's a matter of judging the individual magnetic moments, and pushing aside the—"

"Never mind the explanation," Karn said weakly. "I know how it's done. But I didn't know Earthers could autokineticize."

"We haven't been doing it long. I left the Institute five years ago, and I was in the first graduating class. My name is Henrichs, by the way. Are you *really* from another star?"

Karn didn't answer. Terror was sweeping through him, threatening to destabilize him. It was all he could do to hang onto the Earthbody he wore, and not slip back to his own form. And he realized dimly that there was no longer any need for maintaining the pretense, that this was an Earther who could see his real identity, who could autokineticize, who could enter minds as only a Hethivarian could—

Karn's mind reeled. *It must be another world-line,* he thought frantically. *But that's impossible. I checked everything a dozen times.*

He had to know. His mind reached toward the smiling Earther's—and recoiled.

"You can put up a barrier, too?" Karn asked.

"Of course. Can't you?"

"I—will you let me enter your mind?" Karn asked. "What for?"

"I want to find out—find out what universe I'm in,"

he said in a weak, tired voice.

The Earther lifted the barrier. A moment later, Karn wished he hadn't.

He saw the history of Earth laid out neatly for him in the Earther's mind, as neatly as it had been put in via some history course long before. The course of events followed expectation; with a touch of smugness Karn saw that the Treaty of Düsseldorf *had* existed in this world.

The World War had come to a conclusion in 1916. Karn's work had been successful; the pressures of war had been removed from Earth. But war, it seemed, was not the only stimulus to development. Karn absorbed the history of the years after 1916 with steadily mounting disbelief.

The Earthers had settled down to lives of peaceful, quiet contemplation. There had been many technological advances, of course: radio had become a commercially practicable affair early in the 1920s, aviation had been improved, medicine had taken some steps forward. But there was none of the skyrocketing technological achievement of that other world, the one of the Earth satellite programs and atomic power. Atomics was only a hazy concept in the back of the Earther's mind.

But—behind their national barriers, now safeguarded by the just and wise treaty—these Earthers had developed other skills. Mental skills. Someone named Chalmers had developed the techniques of autokinetics; someone named Resslin had perfected direct communication. And—Karn was appalled—these Earthers seemed to have carried the skills of teleportation to heights undreamed-of even in the Hethivarian Network, which had practised the power for centuries. On Hethivar, no one even considered an autokinetic jaunt greater than a single planetary diameter—while these Earthers seemed to have made trips all throughout their own solar system in the past few years.

Was the technique different? Or did these Earthers use the same method, but manage it more efficiently, so that they could teleport greater distances? Karn probed deeper. The technique was the same.

That meant—

"You haven't answered my question," Henrichs said. "Do you really come from another star? We've never really tried hopping as far as even Alpha Centauri yet, but if there's life out there—"

Karn shuddered. It took weeks for him to make the trip from Hethivar to Earth by nullspace drive. And this Earther was talking about an instantaneous autokinetic hop! Inconceivable!

"I'd like to know the name of your star," Henrichs persisted. "Maybe we can visit it someday. We're just at the beginning of this thing, you know, but there's never any telling how far we can travel."

Karn felt the Earther probing at his mind, seeking to know the location of the Hethivarian Network. In sudden terror he slammed down the barrier, but it was too little and too late; he felt the Earther pounce on the information.

"No, you can't—"

Karn let his words die away. The Earther was gone.

Karn left Earth several minutes later, sending a radio message ahead to Hethivar that he was returning with very serious news. And very serious it was, indeed.

His manipulations of 1916 had worked out well—too well. Much too well. He had throttled Terran technology so splendidly that their innate drive had forced them to a breakthrough in another, and even more dangerous, field.

Teleportation for billions of miles. Unstoppable entry into ships supposedly invisible. Mental barriers that could not be broken. The thought of what these Earthers had accomplished in a few years' time chilled him—especially when he thought of the years that lay ahead.

He fell into morbid brooding on the return voyage. He realized now that it had been futile to attempt to manipulate the Earthers at all. In that other probability world, his alter ego had conceded the futility of holding the Earthers back, and instead was encouraging them, leading them on to the normal mechanical conquest of space.

Karn and his world had tried a different method, and succeeded so well that they had perhaps hastened their own downfall by centuries. He pictured a cosmos full of these Terrans, jaunting from world to world while the Hethivarians lumbered along to clumsy nullspace ships—

It took six weeks for him to reach his home world again. From fifty thousand miles up it looked magnificent; he thrilled at the sight of the sweeping pastel-shaded towers standing nobly in the red-and-gold sunlight of midafternoon. He thumbed for direct contact with the Planners. At this distance, telepathy was impossible for him; he would have to radio.

Adric answered, "About time we heard from you, Karn."

"A thousand pardons, Esteemed One. But the news I bring—frightful! Despite our best attempt at holding them back, the Earthers have reached space anyway." Karn scowled glumly. He and all his people had failed. But had the task been possible in the first place? Perhaps the Earthers, driven by some force beyond all logic, could not *have* been held back. Trying to stop them was like attempting to hold back the sea with a toothpick. "They've developed some form of autokinetics that lets them travel huge distances," Karn went on. "I greatly fear—"

Adric interrupted acidly. "Karn, you blitherer, shut up and bring your ship down to land!"

"Esteemed One, I hope you don't blame *me* for—"

"I'm not blaming anyone for what happened," Adric said. The Noble Planner sounded tired, weary, defeated.

"But what you're telling me isn't any news. I know all about it."

"You know—"

"Yes," the Planner said. "The first Terran ambassador showed up here five weeks ago. He didn't need a ship to get here." In an expressionless voice the highest lord of the Hethivarian Network said, "We signed a Treaty of Friendship with the Earthers weeks ago. We signed it on *their* terms."

THE SHADOW OF WINGS

The children came running towards him, laughing and shouting, up from the lakeside to the spot on the grassy hill where he lay reading; and as Dr. John Donaldson saw what was clutched in the hand of his youngest son, he felt an involuntary tremor of disgust.

"Look, John! Look what Paul caught!" That was his oldest, Joanne. She was nine, a brunette rapidly growing tan on this vacation trip. Behind her came David, eight, fair-haired and lobster-skinned, and in the rear was Paul, the six-year-old, out of breath and gripping in his still pudgy hand a small green frog.

Donaldson shoved his book—Haley, *Studies in Morphological Linguistics*—to one side and sat up. Paul thrust the frog almost into his face. "I saw it hop, John—and I caught it!" He pantomimed the catch with his free hand.

"I saw him do it," affirmed David.

The frog's head projected between thumb and first finger; two skinny webbed feet dangled free at the other end of Paul's hand, while the middle of the unfortunate batrachian was no doubt being painfully compressed by the small clammy hand. Donaldson felt pleased by Paul's display of coordination, unusual for a six-year-old. But at the same time he wished the boy would take the poor frog back to the lake and let it go.

"Paul," he started to say, "you really ought to—"

The direct-wave phone at the far end of the blanket bleeped, indicating that Martha, back at the bungalow, was calling.

"It's Mommy," Joanne said. Somehow they had never cared to call her by her first name, as they did him. "See what she wants, John."

Donaldson sprawled forward and activated the phone. "Martha?"

"John, there's a phone call for you from Washington. I told them you were down by the lake, but they say it's important and they'll hold on."

Donaldson frowned. "Who from Washington?"

"Caldwell, he said. Bureau of Extraterrestrial Affairs. Said it was urgent."

Sighing, Donaldson said, "Okay, I'm coming."

He looked at Joanne and said, as if she hadn't heard the conversation at all, "There's a call for me and I have to go to the cottage to take it. Make sure your brothers don't go into the water while I'm gone. And see that Paul lets that confounded frog go."

Picking up his book, he levered himself to his feet and set out for the phone in the bungalow at a brisk trot.

Caldwell's voice was crisp and efficient and not at all apologetic as he said, "I'm sorry to have to interrupt you during your vacation, Dr. Donaldson. But it's an urgent matter and they tell us you're the man who can help us."

"Perhaps I am. Just exactly what is it you want?"

"Check me if I'm wrong on the background. You're professor of Linguistics at Columbia, a student of the Kethlani languages and author of a study of Kethlani linguistics published in 2087."

"Yes, yes, that's all correct. But—"

"Dr. Donaldson, we've captured a live Kethlan. He entered the System in a small ship and one of our patrol vessels grappled him in, ship and all. We've got him here in Washington and we want you to come talk to him."

For an instant Donaldson was too stunned to react. A live Kethlan? That was like saying, We've found a live Sumerian, or, We've found a live Etruscan.

The Kethlani languages were precise, neat and utterly dead. At one time in the immeasurable past the Kethlani had visited the Solar System. They had left records of their visit on Mars and Venus, in two languages. One of the languages was translatable, because the Martians had translated it into their own, and the Martian language was still spoken as it had been a hundred thousand years before.

Donaldson had obtained his doctorate with what was hailed as a brilliant Rosetta Stone type analysis of the Kethlani language. But a *live* Kethlan? Why—

After a moment he realized he was staring stupidly at his unevenly tanned face in the mirror above the phone cabinet, and that the man on the other end of the wire was making impatient noises.

Slowly he said, "I can be in Washington this afternoon, I guess. Give me some time to pack up my things. You won't want me for long, will you?"

"Until we're through talking to the Kethlan," Caldwell said.

"All right," Donaldson said. "I can take a vacation any time. Kethlani don't come along that often."

He hung up and peered at his face in the mirror. He had had curly reddish hair once, but fifteen years of the academic life had worn his forehead bare. His eyes were mild, his nose narrow and unemphatic, his lips thin and pale. As he studied himself, he did not think he looked very impressive. He looked professional. That was to be expected.

"Well?" Martha asked.

Donaldson shrugged. "They captured some kind of alien spaceship with a live one aboard. And it seems I'm the only person who can speak the language. They want me right away."

"You're going?"

"Of course. It shouldn't take more than a few days. You can manage with the children by yourself, can't you? I mean—"

She smiled faintly, walked around behind him and kneaded the muscle of his sun-reddened back in an affectionate gesture. "I know better than to argue," she said. "We can take a vacation next year."

He swivelled his left hand behind his back, caught her hand and squeezed it fondly. He knew she would never object. After all, his happiness was her happiness—and he was never happier than when working in his chosen field. The phone call today would probably lead to all sorts of unwanted and unneeded publicity for him. But it would also bring him academic success, and there was no denying the genuine thrill of finding out how accurate his guesses about Kethlani pronunciation were.

"You'd better go down to the lake and get the children," he said. "I'll want to say good-bye before I leave."

They had the ship locked in a stasis field in the basement of the Bureau of ET Affairs Building, on Constitution Avenue just across from the National Academy of Sciences. The great room looked like nothing so much as a crypt, Donaldson thought as he entered. Beam projectors were mounted around the walls, focusing a golden glow on the ship. Caught in the field, the ship hovered in midair, a slim, strange-looking torpedolike object about forty feet long and ten feet across the thickest space. A tingle rippled up Donaldson's spine as he saw the Kethlani cursives painted in blue along the hull. He translated them reflexively: *Bringer of Friendship*.

"That's how we knew it was a Kethlani ship," Caldwell said, at his side. He was a small, intense man who hardly reached Donaldson's shoulder; he was Associate Director of the Bureau, and in his superior's absence he was running the show.

Donaldson indicated the projectors. "How come the gadgetry? Couldn't you just sit the ship on the floor instead of floating it that way?"

"That ship's heavy," Caldwell said. "Might crack the floor. Anyway, it's easier to maneuver this way. We can raise or lower the ship, turn it, float it in or out of the door."

"I see," Donaldson said. "And you say there's a live Kethlan in there?"

Caldwell nodded. He jerked a thumb toward a miniature broadcasting station at the far end of the big room. "We've been in contact with him. He talks to us and we talk to him. But we don't understand a damned bit of it, of course. You want to try?"

Donaldson shook his head up and down in a tense affirmative. Caldwell led him down to the radio set, where an eager-looking young man in military uniform sat making adjustments.

Caldwell said, "This is Dr. Donaldson of Columbia. He wrote the definitive book on Kethlani languages. He wants to talk to our friend in there."

A microphone was thrust into Donaldson's hands. He looked at it blankly, then at the pink face of the uniformed man, then at the ship. The inscription was in Kethlani A language, for which Donaldson was grateful. There were two Kethlani languages, highly dissimilar, which he had labelled A and B. He knew his way around in A well enough, but his mastery of Kethlani B was still exceedingly imperfect.

"How do I use this thing?"

"You push the button on the handle, and talk. That's all. The Kethlan can hear you. Anything he says will be picked up here." He indicated a tape recorder and a speaker on the table.

Donaldson jabbed down on the button, and, feeling a strange sense of disorientation, uttered two words in greeting in Kethlani A.

The pronunciation, of course, was sheer guesswork. Donaldson had worked out what was to him a convincing Kethlani phonetic system, but whether that bore any relation to fact remained to be seen.

He waited a moment. Then the speaker emitted a series of harsh, unfamiliar sounds—and, buried in them like gems in a kitchen midden, Donaldson detected familiar-sounding words.

"Speak slowly," he said in Kethlani A. "I . . . have only a few words."

The reply came about ten seconds later, in more measured accents. "How . . . do . . . you . . . speak our language?"

Donaldson fumbled in his small vocabulary for some way of explaining that he had studied Kethlani documents left behind on Mars centuries earlier, and compared them with their understandable Martian translations until he had pried some sense out of them.

He glimpsed the pale, sweat-beaded faces of the ET men around him; they were mystified, wondering what he was saying to the alien but not daring to interrupt. Donaldson felt a flash of pity for them. Until today the bureau had concerned itself with petty things: import of Martian antiquities, study visas for Venus, and the like. Now, suddenly, they found themselves staring at an extra-solar spaceship, and all the giant problems that entailed.

"Find out why he came to the Solar System," Caldwell whispered.

"I'm trying to," Donaldson murmured with some irritation. He said in Kethlani, "You have made a long journey."

"Yes . . . and alone."

"Why have you come?"

There was a long moment of silence; Donaldson waited, feeling tension of crackling intensity starting to build within him. The unreality of the situation obsessed him. He had been fondly confident that he would never have the opportunity to speak actual Kethlani, and that confidence was being shattered.

Finally: "I . . . have come . . . why?"

The inversion was grammatically correct. "Yes," Donaldson said. "Why?"

Another long pause. Then the alien said something which Donaldson did not immediately understand. He asked for a repeat.

It made little sense—but, of course, his Kethlani vocabulary was a shallow one, and he had additional difficulty in comprehending because he had made some mistakes in interpreting vowel values when constructing his Kethlani phonetics.

But the repeat came sharp and clear, and there was no mistaking it.

"I do . . . do not like to talk in this way. Come inside my ship and we will talk there."

"What's he saying?" Caldwell prodded.

Shaken, Donaldson let the mike dangle from limp fingers. "He—he says he wants me to come inside the ship. He doesn't like long-distance conversations."

Caldwell turned at a right angle and said to a waiting assistant. "All right. Have Matthews reverse the stasis field and lower the ship. We're going to give the Kethlan some company."

Donaldson blinked. "Company? You mean you're sending me in there?"

"I sure as hell do mean that. The Kethlan said it's the only way he'd talk, didn't he? And that's what you're here for. To talk to him. So why shouldn't you go in there, eh?"

"Well—look, Caldwell, suppose it isn't safe?"

"If I thought it was risky, I wouldn't send you in," Caldwell said blandly.

Donaldson shook his head. "But look—I don't want to seem cowardly, but I've got three children to think about. I'm not happy about facing an alien being inside his own ship, if you get me."

"I get you," said Caldwell tiredly. "All right. You want to go home? You want to call the whole business off right here and now?"

"Of course not. But——"

"But then you'll have to go in."

"How will I be able to breathe?"

"The alien air is close enough to our own. He's used to more carbon dioxide and less oxygen, but he can handle our air. There's no problem. And no risk. We had a man in there yesterday when the Kethlan opened the outer lock. You won't be in any physical danger. The alien won't bother you."

"I hope not," Donaldson said. He felt hesitant about it; he hadn't bargained on going inside any extra solar spaceships. But they were clustered impatiently around him, waiting to send him inside, and he didn't seem to have much choice. He sensed a certain contempt for him on their faces already. He didn't want to increase their distaste.

"Will you go in?" Caldwell asked.

"All right. All right. Yes. I'll go in."

Nervously Donaldson picked up the microphone and clamped a cold finger over the control button.

"Open your lock," he said to the alien being. "I'm coming inside."

There was a moment's delay while the stasis field projectors were reversed, lowering the ship gently to floor level. As soon as it touched, a panel in the gleaming golden side of the ship rolled smoothly open, revealing an inner panel.

Donaldson moistened his lips, handed the microphone to Caldwell and walked uncertainly forward. He reached the lip of the airlock, stepped up over it and into the ship. Immediately the door rolled shut behind him, closing him into a chamber about seven feet high and four feet wide, bordered in front and back by the outer and inner doors of the lock.

He waited. Had he been claustrophobic he would have been hysterical by now. *But I never would have come in here in the first place then,* he thought.

He waited. More than a minute passed; then, finally, the blank wall before him rolled aside, and the ship was open to him at last. He entered.

At first it seemed to him the interior was totally dark. Gradually, his retinal rods conveyed a little information.

A dim light flickered at one end of the narrow tubular ship. He could make out a few things: rows of reinforcing struts circling the ship at regular spaced distances; a kind of control panel with quite thoroughly alien-looking instruments on it; a large chamber at one end which might be used for storage of food.

But where's the alien? Donaldson wondered.

He turned, slowly, through a three hundred sixty degree rotation, squinting in the dimness. A sort of mist hung before his eyes; the alien's exhalation, perhaps. But he saw no sign of the Kethlan. There was a sweetish, musky odor in the ship, unpleasant though not unbearable.

"Everything okay?" Caldwell's voice said in his earphones.

"So far. But I can't find the alien. It's damnably dark in here."

"Look up," Caldwell advised. "You'll find him. Took our man a while too, yesterday."

Puzzled, Donaldson raised his head and stared into

the gloom-shrouded rafters of the ship, wondering what he was supposed to see. In Kethlani he said loudly, "Where are you? I see you not."

"I am here," came the harsh voice, from above.

Donaldson looked. Then he backed away, double-taking, and looking again.

A great shaggy thing hung head down against the roof of the ship. Staring intently, Donaldson made out a blunt, piggish face with flattened nostrils and huge flaring ears; the eyes, bright yellow but incredibly tiny, glittered with the unmistakable light of intelligence. He saw a body about the size of a man, covered with darkish thick fur and terminating in two short, thick, powerful-looking legs. As he watched the Kethlan shivered and stretched forth its vast leathery wings. In the darkness, Donaldson could see the corded muscular arm in the wing, and the very human looking fingers which sprouted from the uppermost part of the wing.

Violent disgust rose in him, compounded from his own general dislike for animals and from the half-remembered Transylvanian folktales that formed part of every child's heritage. He felt sick; he controlled himself only by remembering that he was in essence an ambassador, and any sickness would have disastrous consequences for him and for Earth. He dared not offend the Kethlan.

My God, he thought. *An intelligent bat!*

He managed to stammer out the words for greeting, and the alien responded. Donaldson, looking away, saw the elongated shadow of wings cast across the ship by the faint light at the other end. He felt weak, wobbly-legged; he wanted desperately to dash through the now-closed airlock. But he forced himself to recover balance. He had a job to do.

"I did not expect you to know Kethlani," the alien said. "It makes my job much less difficult."

"And your job is—"

"To bring friendship from my people to yours. To link our worlds in brotherhood."

The last concept was a little muddy to Donaldson; the literal translation he made mentally was *children-of-one-cave,* but some questioning eventually brought over the concept of brotherhood.

His eyes were growing more accustomed to the lighting, now, and he could see the Kethlan fairly well. An ugly brute, no doubt of it—but probably I look just as bad to him, he thought. The creature's wingspread was perhaps seven or eight feet. Donaldson tried to picture a world of the beasts, skies thick with leather-winged commuters on their way to work.

Evolution had made numerous modifications in the bat structure, Donaldson saw. The brain, of course; and the extra fingers, aside from the ones from which the wings had sprouted. The eyes looked weak, in typical bat fashion, but probably there was compensation by way of keen auditory senses.

Donaldson said, "Where is your world?"

"Far from here. I—"

The rest of the answer was unintelligible to Donaldson. He felt savage impatience with his own limited vocabulary; he wished he had worked just a little harder on translating the Syrtis Major documents. Well, it was too late for that now, of course.

Caldwell cut in suddenly from outside. "Well? We're picking up all the jabber. What's all the talk about?"

"Can't you wait till I'm finished?" Donaldson snapped. Then, repenting, he said: "Sorry. Guess I'm jumpy. Seems he's an ambassador from his people, trying to establish friendly relations with us. At least, I think so. I'll tell you more when I know something about it."

Slowly, in fits and starts, the story emerged. Frequently Donaldson had to ask the Kethlan to stop and double back while he puzzled over a word. He had no way of recording any of the new words he was learning, but he had always had a good memory, and he simply tucked them away.

The Kethlani had visited the Solar System many years ago. Donaldson was unable to translate the actual figure, but it sounded like a lot. At that time the Martians were at the peak of their civilization, and Earth was just an untamed wilderness populated by naked primates. The Kethlan wryly admitted that they had written off Earth as a potential place of civilization because a study of the bat population of Earth had proved unpromising. They had never expected the primates to evolve this way.

But now they had returned, thousands of years later. Mars was bleak and its civilization decayed, but the third world had unexpectedly attained a high degree of culture and was welcome to embrace the Kethlani worlds in friendship and amity.

"How many worlds do you inhabit?"

The Kethlan counted to fifteen by ones. "There are many others we do not inhabit, but simply maintain friendly relations with. Yours would be one, we hope."

The conversation seemed to dwindle to a halt. Donaldson had run out of questions to ask, and he was exhausted by the hour-long strain of conversing in an alien language, under these conditions, within a cramped ship, talking to a creature whose physical appearance filled him with loathing and fear.

His head throbbed. His stomach was knotted in pain and sweat made his clothes cling clammily to his body. He started to grope for ways to terminate the interview; then an idea struck him.

He quoted a fragment of a document written in pure Kethlani B.

There was an instant of stunned silence; then the alien asked in tones of unmistakable suspicion, "Where did you learn that language?"

"I haven't really learned it. I just know a few words."

He explained that he had found examples of both Kethlani A and Kethlani B along with their Martian equivalents; he had worked fairly comprehensively on the A language, but had only begun to explore the B recently.

The Kethlan seemed to accept that. Then it said: "That is not a Kethlani language."

Surprised, Donaldson uttered the interrogative expletive.

The Kethlan said, "It is the language of our greatest enemies, our rivals, our bitter foes. It is the Thygnor tongue."

"But—why did we find your language and the other side by side, then?"

After a long pause the alien said, "Once Thygnor and Kethlan were friends. Long ago we conducted a joint expedition to this sector of space. Long ago, before the rivalry sprang up. But now"—the alien took on a sorrowful inflection—"now we are enemies."

That explained a great many things, Donaldson realized. The differences between Kethlani A and Kethlani B had been too great for it to seem as if one race spoke both of them. But a joint expedition—that made it understandable.

"Some day, perhaps, the Thygnor will visit your world. But by then you will be on guard against them."

"What do they look like?"

The alien described them, and Donaldson listened and was revolted. As far as he could understand, they were giant intelligent toads, standing erect, amphibian but warm-blooded, vile-smelling, their bodies exuding a nauseous thick secretion.

Giant toads, bats, the lizards of Mars—evidently the primate monopoly of intelligence was confined solely to Earth, Donaldson realized. It was a humbling thought. His face wrinkled in displeasure at the mental image of the toad people the Kethlan had created for him, as he recalled the harmless little frog Paul had captured by the lake.

He spoke in English, attracting Caldwell's attention, and explained the situation.

"He wants me to swear brotherhood with him. He also says there's another intelligent race with interstellar travel—toads, no less—and that they're likely to pay us a visit some day too. What should I do?"

"Go ahead and swear brotherhood," Caldwell said after a brief pause. "It can't hurt. We can always unswear it later, if we like. Say we had our fingers crossed while we were doing it, or something. Then when the frogs get here we can find out which bunch is better for us to be in league with."

The cynicism of the reply annoyed Donaldson, but it was not his place to raise any objections. He said to the alien, "I am prepared to pledge brotherhood between Earth and the Kethlan worlds."

The Kethlan fluttered suddenly down from its perch with a rustle of great wings, and stood facing Donaldson, tucking its wings around its thick shaggy body. Alarmed, Donaldson stepped back.

The alien said reassuringly, "The way we pledge is by direct physical embrace, symbolizing harmony and friendship across the cosmos." He unfurled his wings. "Come close to me."

No! Donaldson shrieked inwardly, as the mighty wings rose high and wrapped themselves about him. *Go away! Don't touch me!* He could smell the sweet, musky smell of the alien, feel its furry warmth, hear the mighty heart pounding, pounding in that massive rib cage...

Revulsion dizzied him. He forced himself to wrap his arms around the barrel of a body while the wings blanketed him, and they stood that way for a moment, locked in a tight embrace.

At length the alien released him. "Now we are friends.

It is only the beginning of a long and fruitful relationship between our peoples. I hope to speak with you again before long."

It was a dismissal. On watery legs Donaldson tottered forward toward the opening airlock, pausing only to mutter a word of farewell before he stumbled through and out into the arms of the waiting men outside.

"Well?" Caldwell demanded. "What happened? Did you swear brotherhood?"

"Yes," Donaldson said wearily. "I swore." The stench of the alien clung to him, sweet in his nostrils. It was as though throbbing wings still enfolded him. "I'm leaving now," he said. "I still have a little of my vacation left. I want to take it."

He gulped a drink that someone handed him. He was shaking and grey-faced, but the effect of the embrace was wearing off. *Only an irrational phobia,* he told himself. *I shouldn't be reacting this way.*

But already he was beginning to forget the embrace of the Kethlan, and the rationalization did him no good. A new and more dreadful thought was beginning to develop within him.

He was the only Terrestrial expert on Kethlani B, too—the Thygnor tongue. And some day, perhaps soon, the Thygnor were going to come to Earth, and Caldwell was going to impress him into service as an interpreter again.

He wondered how the toad people pledged eternal brotherhood.

ABSOLUTELY INFLEXIBLE

The detector over in one corner of Mahler's little office gleamed a soft red. With a weary gesture of his hand he drew it to the attention of the sad-eyed time jumper who sat slouched glumly across the desk from him, looking cramped and uncomfortable in his bulky spacesuit.

"You see," Mahler said, tapping his desk. "They've just found another one. We're constantly bombarded with you people. When you get to the Moon, you'll find a whole Dome full of them. I've sent over four thousand there myself since I took over the bureau. And that was over eight years ago—in twenty-seven twenty-six, to be exact. An average of five hundred a year. Hardly a day goes by without someone dropping in on us."

"And not one has been set free," the time jumper said. "Every time traveller who's come here has been packed off to the Moon immediately. Every single one."

"Every one," Mahler agreed. He peered through the thick shielding, trying to see what sort of man was hidden inside the spacesuit.

Mahler often wondered about the men he condemned

so easily to the Moon. This one was small in stature, with wispy locks of white hair pasted to his high forehead by perspiration. Evidently he had been a scientist, a respected man of his time, perhaps a happy father—although very few of the time jumpers were family men. Perhaps he possessed some bit of scientific knowledge which would be invaluable to the 28th Century. Or perhaps he didn't. It scarcely mattered. Like all the rest, he would have to be sent to the Moon, to live out his remaining days under the grueling, primitive conditions of the Dome.

"Don't you think that's a little cruel?" the other asked. "I came here with no malice, no intent to harm anyone. I'm simply a scientific observer from the past. Driven by curiosity, I took the Jump. I never expected that I'd be walking into life imprisonment."

"I'm sorry," Mahler said, getting up.

He decided to end the interview then and there. He had to get rid of this jumper because there was another space traveller coming right up. Some days they came thick and fast, and this looked like one of the really bad days. But the efficient mechanical tracers never missed a jumper.

"But can't I live on Earth and stay in this spacesuit?" the man asked, panicky now that he saw his interview with Mahler was coming to an end. "That way I'd be sealed off from contact at all times."

"Please don't make this any harder than it is for me," Mahler said. "I've explained to you why we must be absolutely inflexible. There cannot—must not—be any exceptions. Two centuries have now passed since the last outbreak of disease on Earth. So naturally we've lost most of the resistance acquired over the countless generations when disease was rampant. I'm risking my life coming so close to you, even with the spacesuit sealing you off."

Mahler signalled to the tall, powerful guards who were

waiting in the corridor, looking like huge, heavily ar-
mored beetles in the casings that protected them from
infection. This was always the worst moment.

"Look," Mahler said, frowning with impatience.
"You're a walking death trap. You probably carry enough
disease germs to kill half the world. Even a cold—a
common cold—would wipe out millions now. Acquired
immunity to disease has simply vanished over the past
two centuries. It's no longer needed, with all diseases
conquered. But you time travellers show up loaded with
potentialities for all the diseases that once wiped out
whole populations. And we can't risk having you stay
here with them."

"But I'd—"

"I know. You'd swear by all that's holy to you or to
me that you'd never leave the confines of the spacesuit.
Sorry. The word of the most honorable man doesn't
carry any weight against the safety of two billion human
lives. We can't take the slightest risk by letting you stay
on Earth.

"I know. It's unfair, it's cruel—it's anything else you
may choose to call it. You had no idea you would walk
into a situation like this. Well, I feel sorry for you. But
you knew you were going on a one-way trip to the future,
and would be subject to whatever that future might decide
to do with you. You knew that you could not possibly
return in time to your own age."

Mahler began to tidy up the paper on his desk with a
brusqueness that signalled finality. "I'm terribly sorry,
but you'll just have to try to understand our point of
view," he said. "We're frightened to death by your very
presence here. We can't allow you to roam Earth, even
in a spacesuit. No. There's nothing for you but the Moon.
I have to be absolutely inflexible. Take him away," he
said gesturing to the guards.

They advanced on the little man and began gently to
ease him out of Mahler's office.

Mahler sank gratefully into the pneumochair and sprayed his throat with laryngogel. These long speeches always left him exhausted, and now his throat felt raw and scraped. *Someday I'll get throat cancer from all this talking.* Mahler thought. *And that'll mean the nuisance of an operation. But if I don't do this job, someone else will have to.*

Mahler heard the protesting screams of the time jumper impassively. In the beginning he had been ready to resign on first witnessing the inevitable frenzied reaction of jumper after jumper as the guards dragged them away. But eight years had hardened him.

They had given him the job because he had been a hard man in the first place. It was a job that called for a hard man. Condrin, his predecessor, had not been the same sort of man at all, and because of his tragic weakness Condrin was now himself on the Moon. He had weakened after heading the bureau a year, and had let a jumper go.

The jumper had promised to secrete himself at the tip of Antarctica and Condrin, thinking that Antarctica would be as safe as the Moon, had foolishly released him. Right after that they had called Mahler in. In eight years Mahler had sent four thousand men to the Moon. The first had been the runaway jumper—intercepted in Buenos Aires after he had left a trail of disease down the hemisphere from Appalachia to the Argentine Protectorate. The second had been Condrin.

It was getting to be a tiresome job, Mahler thought. But he was proud to hold it and be in a position to save millions of lives. It took a strong man to do what he was doing. He leaned back and awaited the arrival of the next jumper.

Instead the door slid smoothly open, and the burly body of Dr. Fournet, the bureau's chief medical man, broke the photoelectric beam. Mahler glanced up. Fournet carried a time rig dangling from one hand.

"I took this away from our latest customer," Fournet said. "He told the medic who examined him that it was a two-way rig and I thought you'd better be the first to look it over."

Mahler came to full attention quickly. A two-way rig? Unlikely, he thought. But if it was true it would mean the end of the dreary jumper prison on the Moon. Only how could a two-way rig exist? He reached out and took the rig from Fournet.

"It seems to be a conventional twenty-fourth century type," he said.

"But notice the extra dial," Fournet said, frowning.

Mahler peered and nodded. "Yes. It *seems* to be a two-way rig, all right. But how can we test it? And it's not really very probable," he added. "Why should a two-way rig suddenly show up from the twenty-fourth century, when no other traveller has one? We don't even have two-way time travel ourselves, and our scientists insist that we never will.

"Still," he mused, "it's a nice thing to dream about. We'll have to study this a little more closely. But I don't seriously think it will work. Bring the jumper in, will you?"

As Fournet turned to signal the guards, Mahler asked him, "What's the man's medical report, by the way?"

"From here to here," Fournet said somberly. "You name it, he's carrying it. Better get him shipped off to the Moon as quickly as you can. I won't feel safe until he's off this planet."

The big medic waved to the guards.

Mahler smiled. Fournet's overcautiousness was proverbial in the Bureau. Even if a jumper were to show up completely free from disease, Fournet would probably insist that he was carrying everything from asthma to leprosy.

The guards brought the jumper into Mahler's office. He was fairly tall, Mahler saw—and quite young. It was difficult to see his face clearly through the dim plate of the protective spacesuit which all jumpers were compelled to wear. But Mahler could tell that the young time traveller's face had much of the lean, hard look of Mahler's own. It was just possible that the jumper's eyes had widened in surprise as he entered the office, but Mahler could not be sure.

"I never dreamed I'd find *you* here," the jumper said. The transmitter of the spacesuit brought the young man's voice over deeply and resonantly. "Your name is Mahler, isn't it?"

"That's right," Mahler conceded.

"To go all these years—and find *you*. Talk about wild improbabilities!"

Mahler ignored him, declining to take up the challenge. He had found it to be good practice never to let a captured jumper get the upper hand in conversation. His standard procedure was firmly to explain to the jumper just why it was imperative for him to be sent to the Moon, and then to summon the guards as quickly as possible.

"You say this is a two-way time rig?" Mahler asked, holding up the flimsy-looking piece of equipment.

"That's right," the other agreed. "It works both ways. If you pressed the button you'd go straight back to the year two thousand, three hundred and sixty, or thereabouts."

"Did you build it?"

"Me? No, hardly," said the jumper. "I found it. It's a long story and I don't have time to tell it now. In fact, if I tried to tell it I'd only make things ten times worse than they are. No. Let's get this over with as quickly as we can, shall we? I know I don't stand much of a chance with you, and I'd just as soon make it quick."

"You know, of course, that this is a world without disease—" Mahler began sonorously.

"And that you think I'm carrying enough germs of different sorts to wipe out the whole world. And therefore you have to be absolutely inflexible with me. All right. I won't try to argue with you. Which way is the Moon?"

Absolutely inflexible. The phrase Mahler had used so many times, the phrase that summed him up so neatly! He chuckled to himself. Some of the younger technicians must have tipped off the jumper about the usual procedure, and the jumper had resigned himself to going peacefully, without bothering to plead. It was just as well.

Absolutely inflexible.

Yes, Mahler thought, the words fitted him well. He was becoming a stereotype in the Bureau. Perhaps he was the only Bureau Chief who had never relented, and let a jumper go. Probably all of the others, bowed under the weight of hordes of curious men flooding in from the past, had finally cracked and taken the risk.

But not Mahler—not Absolutely Inflexible Mahler. He took pride in the deep responsibility that rode on his shoulders, and had no intention of evading a sacred trust. His job was to find the jumpers and get them off Earth as quickly and as efficiently as possible. Every single one. It was a task that required relentless inflexibility.

"This makes my job much easier," Mahler said. "I'm glad I won't have to convince you that I am simply doing my duty."

"Not at all," the other said. "I understand. I won't even waste my breath. The task you must carry out is understandable, and I cannot hope to make you change your mind." He turned to the guards. "I'm ready. Take me away."

Mahler gestured to them, and they led the jumper away. Amazed, Mahler watched the retreating figure, studying him until he could no longer be seen.

If they were all like that, Mahler thought. *I could have gotten to like that one. He was a sensible man—one of the few. He knew he was beaten, and he didn't try to argue in the face of absolute necessity. It's too bad he had to go. He's the kind of man I'd like to find more*

*often these days. But I mustn't feel sympathy. That would
be unwise.*

Mahler had succeeded as an administrator only because he had managed to suppress any sympathy for the
unfortunates he had been compelled to condemn. Had
there been any other place to send them—back to their
own time, preferably—he would have been the first to
urge abolition of the Moon prison. But, with only one
course of action open to him, he performed his job efficiently and automatically.

He picked up the jumper's time rig and examined it.
A two-way rig would be the solution, of course. As soon
as the jumper arrived, a new and better policy would be
in force, turning him around and sending him back. They'd
get the idea quickly enough. Mahler found himself wish-
ing it could be so; he often wondered what the jumpers
stranded on the Moon must think of him.

A two-way rig would change the world so completely
that its implications would be staggering. With men able
to move at will backward and forward in time the past,
present, and future would blend into one broad and shin-
ing highway. It was impossible to conceive of the world
as it might be, with free passage in either direction.

But even as Mahler fondled the confiscated time rig
he realized that something was wrong. In the six centuries
since the attainment of time travel, no one had yet developed a known two-way rig. And an unknown rig was
pretty well ruled out. There were no documented reports
of visitors from the future and presumably, if such a rig
existed, such visitors would have been as numerous as
were the jumpers from the past.

So the young man had been lying, Mahler thought
with regret. The two-way rig was an utter impossibility.
The youth had merely been playing a game with his
captors. There *couldn't* be a two-way rig, because the
past had never been in any way influenced by the future.

Mahler examined the rig. There were two dials on

it—the conventional forward dial and another indicating backward travel. Whoever had prepared the incredible hoax had gone to considerable trouble to document it. *Why?*

Could it be that the jumper had been telling the truth? Mahler wished that he could somehow test the rig immediately. There was always the one slim chance that it might actually work, and that he would no longer have to be a rigid dispenser of justice. Absolutely Inflexible Mahler!

He looked at it. As a time machine, it was fairly crude. It made use of the standard distorter pattern, but the dial was the clumsy wide-range 24th-Century one. The vernier system, Mahler reflected, had not been introduced until the 25th Century.

Mahler peered closer to read the instruction label. PLACE LEFT HAND HERE, it said. He studied it carefully. The ghost of a thought wandered into his mind. He pushed it aside in horror, but it recurred. It would be so simple. What if he should—

No.

But—

PLACE LEFT HAND HERE.

He reached out tentatively with his left hand.

Be careful now. No sense in being reckless—

PLACE LEFT HAND HERE.

PRESS DIAL.

He placed his left hand lightly on the indicated place. There was a little crackle of electricity. He let go, quickly, and started to replace the time rig when the desk abruptly faded out from under him.

The air was foul and grimy. Mahler wondered what had happened to the Conditioner. Then he looked around.

Huge, grotesque, ugly buildings blocked out most of the sky. There were dark oppressive clouds of smoke overhead, and the harsh screech of an industrial society assailed his ears.

He was in the middle of an immense city, and streams of people were rushing past him at a furious pace. They were all small, stunted creatures, their faces harried and neurotic. They all had the same despairing, frightened look. It was an expression Mahler had seen many times on the faces of jumpers escaping from an unendurable nightmare world to a more congenial future.

He stared down at the time rig clutched in his hand, and knew what had happened. The two-way rig!

It meant the end of the Moon prisons. It meant a complete revolution in civilization. But he had no desire to remain in so oppressive and horrible an age a minute longer than was necessary. He reached down to activate the time rig.

Abruptly someone jolted him from behind and the current of the crowd swept him along. He was struggling desperately to regain control over himself when a hand reached out and gripped the back of his neck.

"Got a card, Hump?" a harsh voice demanded.

He whirled to face an ugly, squinting-eyed man in a dull-brown uniform.

"Did you hear what I said? Where's your card, Hump? Talk up or you get Spotted."

Mahler twisted out of the man's grasp and started to jostle his way quickly through the crowd, desiring nothing more than an opportunity to set the time rig and get out of this disease-ridden, squalid era forever. As he shoved people out of his way they shouted angrily and tried to trip him, raining blows on his back and shoulders.

"There's a Hump!" someone called. "Spot him!"

The cry became a roar. "Spot him! Spot him! Spot him!"

He turned left and went pounding down a side street, and now it was a full-fledged mob that dashed after him, shouting in savage fury.

"Send for the Crimers!" a deep voice boomed. "They'll Spot him!"

A running man caught up to him and in sheer desperation Mahler swung about and let fly with his fists. He heard a dull grunt of pain, but he did not pause in his headlong flight. The unaccustomed exercise was tiring him rapidly.

An open door beckoned, and he hurried swiftly toward it.

An instant later he was inside a small furniture shop and a salesman was advancing toward him. "Can I help you, sir? The latest models, right here."

"Just leave me alone," Mahler panted, squinting at the time rig.

The salesman stared uncomprehendingly as Mahler fumbled with the little dial.

There was no vernier. He'd have to chance it and hope to hit the right year. The salesman suddenly screamed and came to life—for reasons Mahler would never understand.

Mahler ignored him and punched the stud viciously.

It was wonderful to step back into the serenity of 28th-Century Appalachia. It was small wonder so many time jumpers came to so peaceful an age, Mahler reflected, as he waited for his overworked heart to calm down. Almost anything would be preferable to *back there*.

He looked up and down the quiet street, seeking a Convenience where he could repair the scratches and bruises he had acquired during his brief stay in the past. They would scarcely be able to recognize him at the bureau in his present battered condition, with one eye nearly closed, and a great livid welt on his cheek.

He sighted one at last and started down the street, only to be brought up short by the sound of a familiar soft mechanical whining. He looked around to see one of the low-running mechanical tracers of the bureau purring up the street toward him. It was closely followed by two bureau guards, clad in their protective casings.

Of course! He had arrived from the past, and the

detectors had recorded his arrival, just as they would have pinpointed any time traveller. They never missed.

He turned, and walked toward the guards. He failed to recognize them, but this did not surprise him. The bureau was a vast and wide-ranging organization, and he knew only a handful of the many guards who customarily accompanied the tracers. It was a pleasant relief to see the tracer. The use of tracers had been instituted during his adminstration, and he was absolutely sure now that he hadn't returned too early along the time stream.

"Good to see you," he called to the approaching guards. "I had a little accident in the office."

They ignored him, and began methodically to unpack a spacesuit from the storage trunk of the mechanical tracer.

"Never mind talking," one said. "Get into this."

He paled. "But I'm no jumper," he protested. "Hold on a moment, fellows. This is all a terrible mistake. I'm Mahler—head of the bureau. *Your boss.*"

"Don't play games with us, chum," the tall guard said, while the other forced the spacesuit down over Mahler's shoulders. To his horror, Mahler saw that they did not recognize him at all.

"Suppose you just come peacefully and let the chief explain everything to you, without any trouble," the short guard said.

"But I *am* the chief," Mahler protested. "I was examining a two-way rig in my office and accidentally sent myself back to the past. Take this thing off me and I'll show you my identification card. That should convince you."

"Look, chum, we don't want to be convinced of anything. Tell it to the chief, if you like. Now, are you coming—or do we bring you?"

There was no point, Mahler decided, in trying to prove his identity to the clean-faced young medic who examined him at the bureau office. To insist on an immediate

identification would only add more complications. No.
It would be far better to wait until he reached the office
of the chief.

He knew now what had happened. Apparently he had
landed somewhere in his own future, shortly after his
own death. Someone else had taken over the bureau, and
he, Mahler had been forgotten. He suddenly realized with
a little shock that at that very moment his ashes were
probably reposing in an urn at the Appalachia Crema-
torium.

When he got to the chief of the bureau, he would
simply and calmly explain exactly what had happened
and ask for permission to go back ten or twenty or thirty
years to the time in which he belonged. Once there, he
could turn the two-way rig over to the proper authorities
and resume his life from his point of departure. When
that happened, the jumpers would no longer be sent to
the Moon, and there would be no further need for Inflexible Mahler.

But, he suddenly realized, if he'd already done that
why was there still a clearance bureau? An uneasy fear
began to grow in him.

"Hurry up and finish that report," Mahler told the
medic.

"I don't know what the rush is," the medic complained. "Unless you like it on the Moon."

"Don't worry about me," Mahler said confidently. "If
I told you who I am, you'd think twice about—"

"Is this thing your time rig?" the medic asked unexpectedly.

"Not really. I mean—yes, yes it is," Mahler said.
"And be careful with it. It's the world's only two-way
rig."

"Really, now!" said the medic. "Two ways, eh?"

"Yes. And if you'll take me to your chief—"

"Just a minute. I'd like to show this to the head medic."

In a few moments the medic returned. "All right, we'll

go to the chief now. I'd advise you not to bother arguing with him. You can't win. You should have stayed in your own age."

Two guards appeared and jostled Mahler down the familiar corridor to the brightly lit little office where he had spent eight years of his life. Eight years on the other side of the fence!

As he approached the room that had once been his office, he carefully planned what he would say to his successor. He would explain the accident first, of course. Then he would establish his identity beyond any possibility of doubt and request permission to use the two-way rig to return to his own time. The chief would probably be belligerent at first. But he'd quickly enough become curious, and finally amused at the chain of events that had ensnarled Mahler.

And, of course, he would make amends, after they had exchanged anecdotes about the job they both held at the same time across a wide gap of years. Mahler vowed that he would never again touch a time machine, once he got back. He would let others undertake the huge job of transmitting the jumpers back to their own eras.

He moved forward and broke the photoelectric beam. The door to the bureau chief's office slid open. Behind the desk sat a tall, powerfully built man with hard grey eyes.

Me!

Through the dim plate of the spacesuit into which he had been stuffed, Mahler stared in stunned horror at the man behind the desk. It was impossible for him to doubt that he was gazing at Inflexible Mahler, the man who had sent four thousand men to the Moon, without exception, in the unbending pursuit of his duty.

And if he's Mahler—

Who am I?

Suddenly Mahler saw the insane circle complete. He recalled the jumper, the firm, deep-voiced, unafraid time jumper who had arrived claiming to have a two-way rig and who had marched off to the Moon without arguing. Now Mahler knew who that strange jumper was.

But how did the cycle start? Where had the two-way rig come from in the first place? He had gone to the past to bring it to the present to take it to the past to—

His head swam. There was no way out. He looked at the man behind the desk and began to walk slowly toward him, feeling a wall of circumstance growing up around him, while in frustration he tried impotently to beat his way out.

It was utterly pointless to argue. Not with Absolutely Inflexible Mahler. It would just be a waste of breath. The wheel had come full circle, and he was as good as on the Moon already. He looked at the man behind the desk with a new, strange light in his eyes.

"I never dreamed I'd find you here," the jumper said. The transmitter of the spacesuit brought the jumper's voice over deeply and resonantly.

HIS BROTHER'S WEEPER

The Deserializing Room at Cincinnati Spaceport was, Peter Martlett thought, a little on the bleak side. It was no more than twenty feet square, illuminated by a single hooded fluorobulb, and was bare of all ornament. In the center of the floorspace stood the awesome bulk of the Henderson Deserializer. Two white-smocked technicians flanked it, staring eagerly at Martlett, who had just entered. Behind him sounded the noisy hum of the waiting room he had quitted. There was a lot of deserializing going on today.

"Mr. Martlett?"

Martlett nodded tensely. He was more than a little leery of submitting himself to the Deserializer, especially after what had happened to his brother Michael. But the travel-agency people had assured him that that had been a fluke, one-in-a-million, one-in-a-billion—

"May we have your passport?" said the thinner and more efficient looking of the two technicians. Martlett surrendered it, along with his accident claim waiver, his identification ticket, his departure permit, and the prestamped entrance visa that would allow him to visit Marathon where his brother had gone to a hideous death the month before.

Heads almost touching, the pair of them riffled quickly through Martlett's papers, nodded in agreement, and gestured for him to take a seat in the Deserializer. One of the technicians produced a dark enamelled square box a foot on each side and proceeded to attach Martlett's documents to it with stickons. Moistening his lips, Martlett watched. In a very few minutes, he knew, he himself would be inside the box.

The other deserializing technician strapped Martlett firmly into the Deserializer and lowered a metal cone over his head. In a soothing voice he said, "Of course you understand the approximate nature of the Deserializer, sir—"

"Yes, I—"

Ignoring the outburst, the technician continued what was obviously a memorized speech delivered before each departure. "The Henderson Deserializer makes possible instantaneous traffic between stars. The deserializing field induces distortion of the four coordinate axes of your worldline, removing you temporarily from contact with the temporal axis and—for convenience in storage— somewhat compressing you along the tree spatial axes."

"You mean I'll be put in that little box?"

"Exactly, sir. You and your luggage will enter this container and you will be placed aboard a spaceship bound for the planet of your destination. Ah—Marathon, I believe. Although the journey to Marathon requires two hundred eighty-three objective years, for you it will be a matter of seconds—since, of course, on your arrival you will enter another deserializing field that will restore you to your temporal axis at a point only seconds after you had left it on Earth!"

"In short," the other technician chimed in, "you enter a box here, are shipped to Marathon, and are unpacked there—total elapsed time, ten seconds. If you choose to return to Earth immediately on arrival, you could do that. If you felt like it, you could make nearly thirty round trips a minute, eighteen hundred an hour—"

"If I could afford it," Martlett said dryly. The round trip fare was nine hundred units, and it was making a considerable dent in his savings. But, of course, the Colonial Government of Marathon had asked him to make the trip, to settle his brother's unfinished affairs. And the shock of Michael's tragic death had been such that he had agreed at once to make the trip.

"Heh, heh," chuckled the technician. "To be sure, eighteen hundred round trips *would* be on the costly side! Heh heh heh—"

The two technicians chuckled harmoniously, all the while bustling round Martlett and making adjustments in the complex network of dials and levers that hemmed him in on all sides. He was just beginning to get annoyed at all the laughter when—

Whick!

—he found himself lying on a plush, well-padded couch in a room walled mostly with curving glass. The sun was in his eyes—bluish-purple sunlight. Green-tinted clouds drifted lazily in the auburn sky. Two smiling technicians in sheen-grey coveralls were nodding at him in smug satisfaction.

"Welcome to Marathon, Mr. Martlett."

Martlett licked his lips. "I'm here?"

"You are. Transhipped from Cincinnati Spaceport, Earth, aboard the good ship *Venus*. Today is the 11th of April, 2209, Galactic Standard Time."

"The same day I left Earth!"

"Of course, Mr. Martlett, of course! The Henderson Deserializer—"

"Yes, yes, I know," Martlett interjected hastily, forestalling yet another rendition of the Information for Travellers Speech. "I fully understand the process." He looked around. "I'm here on request of your Secretary for Internal Affairs, Mr. Jansen. It's about my brother—"

The word was ill-chosen. It triggered a strong reaction in the two deserializer men. They coughed and reddened and glanced obliquely over Martlett's head as if they were very embarrassed. Martlett pressed on undisturbed. "My brother Michael, who was a colonist here until his unfortunate death in a Deserializer accident last month. Do you know where I can find the secre—"

"He's waiting outside to see you," said the short technician with the swerving nose.

"And we wish to assure you that this office has been cleared of all responsibility in the matter of your brother's—ah—disappearance," put in the tall one with the unconvincing yellow toupee.

Martlett stared at them sourly. "I'm not here to press charges," he said. "Just to settle my late brother's affairs."

He rose, feeling a bit stiff around the knees. Not surprising, he thought, considering he had just spent two hundred eighty-three objective years in an enamelled box one foot square. Gathering up his papers, he stepped out into the antechamber, discovering as he walked the Marathon's gravity was only about two-thirds that of Earth. It was all he could do to keep himself from skipping. Skipping, he thought, would hardly look decorous on a man whose beloved brother had gone to an untimely death only five Galactic Standard Weeks before.

The Marathonian Secretary for Internal Affairs introduced himself as Octavian Jansen, a fact Martlett already knew. He was a tall, stoop-shouldered man of dignified appearance and middle age. His office, he said, was within walking distance of the Arrivals Center, and so they walked there. Martlett enjoyed the springy sensation of walking at two-thirds grav. He threw his head back, breathing in the clean, fresh air. Overhead, colorful birds wheeled and screeched playfully. Swaying palmoid trees lined the streets. Marathon, Michael had often written to him, was nothing more or less than a paradise. Fertile soil, extravagantly satisfactory climate, so native carnivorous life forms bigger than caninoids and felinoids, and the women!

Yes, the women! Michael had always had a good eye for the women, Martlett reflected.

Jansen's office was handsomely furnished. A brace of hunting trophies loomed on one wall, great lowering massive purple-skinned trihorned heads: Marathon's largest life form, the ponderous, herbivorous, harmless hippopotamoids. Sleek freeform chairs faced the freeform onyx-topped desk. Martlett pulled one up.

Jansen said, "May I remark that you look astonishingly like your late brother, Mr. Martlett?"

"Many people thought we were twins."

"You are the older brother?"

"By three years. I'm 30. Michael is—was—27."

For a moment Jansen's eyes dropped respectfully. "Your brother was very popular here, Mr. Martlett. From the day he joined our colony two years ago, he was a leader of the community. And I needn't tell you how much we admired his music! Only next month our local symphony orchestra was to have presented an all-Martlett concert: the Second Symphony, the Theremin Concerto, and a piece for strings and synthesizer called simply *Amor*."

Martlett nodded. Michael's success here was part of an old story. Michael, no more handsome than he, no taller and no more muscular, had always been the gregarious brother, surrounded by admirers and adored by women. While he, Peter, the older brother and presumably the wiser, was instead regarded as a sort of bumbling foster uncle, not too clever, who needed help in all he undertook. And so it had gone. In a world where a serious composer stood no chance at all against the symphonic computers, Michael had won indelible musical fame at the age of twenty-three. Two years later, he had pocketed a fat fellowship and departed for the pleasant world of Marathon to continue his composing, far from the jarring dissonances of Terran life.

And now, at twenty-seven, he was dead. The older brother, shy, uncertain Peter, had the task of gathering together the reins Michael had abruptly dropped, collecting his belongings, settling his debts.

"Has the concert been cancelled?" Martlett asked.

"Oh, no," Jansen said. "It's being done as a memorial. Your brother was to have conducted himself, but we've hired someone else. It's to be given on the fifteenth of May. I do hope you'll attend."

"Sorry," Martlett said brusquely. "I wasn't planning to stay on Marathon more than a week or two—just long enough to do whatever needs to be done about Michael's affairs. By the middle of May I'll be back on Earth, I'm afraid."

"As you wish, of course." Jansen shrugged mournfully. "I've taken the liberty of assembling a portfolio of bills that your brother left unpaid at the time of his death."

Martlett took the bulky folder from him and opened it. The uppermost bill was from the Marathon Deserialized Instantaneous Transportation Corporation: 110 units charged for a journey from Marathon to the neighboring world of Thermopylae, ten units down and six months to pay.

"I hardly think *this* bill needs to be paid," Martlett said, nudging it across the desk to Jansen.

The secretary looked at it, flushed, and said quickly, "Ah—of course not—an error, Mr. Martlett—"

An error indeed, Martlett thought. That journey had never been completed. Michael had entered the Deserializer on Marathon, and ostensibly was to have arrived on Thermopylae, ninety million miles away, almost at once. But the Deserializer box had been empty when it reached Thermopylae. Somewhere in mid-journey Michael had disappeared, his compressed and deserialized body shunted off irrevocably into some parallel continuum, into that dark bourn from which no traveller returns.

The law in such cases—they were one-in-a-billion occurrences—was plain. The missing party was to be considered legally dead. No one had ever returned who had disappeared in mid-jaunt via Deserializer.

Martlett thumbed through the rest of the bills. They were small ones, but there were plenty of them—a heavy liquor tab, five florists' bills, an invoice from a men's clothier and a larger one from a woman's outfitter, and so on. Evidently Michael had not lost his old touch with the women, Martlett thought.

The total, he computed roughly, was in the vicinity of three thousand units. He could afford the outlay; the royalties from Michael's music, whose performance rights he had automatically inherited, would reimburse him soon enough.

"Very well," Martlett said. "I'll take care of all these matters right away. Now, if there are any other—"

"Yes," Jansen said gravely. "I believe you should know there was a woman. A—well—ah—your brother's fiancée."

"His *what?* Why, Michael used to swear day and night he'd never let himself get trapped into marrying!"

"Be that as it may, this woman claims he made a definite promise to her. I think you ought to pay a call on her—ah—in the interests of good form, you know."

Her name was Sondra Bullard. Martlett went to visit her that evening, after he had finished installing himself in his brother's palmoid-ringed fourteen-room villa. She lived half a continent away—Marathon was somewhat on the sprawling side—and Martlett found it necessary to charter an aircab to get there.

Sondra Bullard's dwelling was modest compared to

Michael's—a ranch-type affair that rambled over a few acres of grassy meadow at the foot of a handsome plunging waterfall. A gleaming jetcar jutted from the open garage. Martlett wondered in passing if Michael had bought her these things. He had always been extravagant.

Feeling a little uneasy, Martlett strode up the flagstoned walk and stepped into the green scanner field that glowed round the door. A chime sounded within, calling Miss Bullard's attention to the fact that she had a visitor; a moment went by, and then a piercing shriek was distinctly audible.

Martlett felt perspiration begin to bead his forehead. Before he could give way completely to alarm and turn to run, the front door opened and Miss Sondra Bullard peered out at him. She was dressed unsurprisingly in black, and her face was astonishingly pale. She was also, Martlett noted, quite lovely. Michael's taste had always been impeccable.

"You're—Michael's—*brother?*"

"That's right. Peter Martlett. I called earlier, you remember."

"Yes. Won't you come in?" She spoke mechanically, chopping each word off into an individual sentence.

Once he was inside she said, "You—look very much like your brother, you know."

"So I've been told."

"I was frightened when I saw your image in the scanner field." She laughed in self-deprecation. "I guess I thought it was Michael at the door. Silly of me, but you two *did* look so much alike. Were you twins?"

"I was three years the elder."

"Oh."

After a few lame moments of silence the girl said, "Drink?"

"Yes, please. Something mild."

She dialed a filtered rum for him and a stiff highball for herself. While he sipped, Martlett surreptitiously looked around. A lot of cash had been tossed into these furnishings, and it seemed to him he recognized his brother's fine hand—and money—in the decorating scheme. He felt a momentary current of anger; this girl, he thought, had been *milking* Michael!

Oh, no, came the immediate inner denial. Michael had been nobody's fool. He wasn't susceptible to gold-digging.

Hesitantly Martlett said, "Secretary Jansen was telling me you knew Michael quite well."

"We were engaged," she said immediately.

Since he had been warned, Martlett was able to avoid the double take. "Odd, Michael never wrote to me about it. Had you known him long?"

"Six months. We became engaged nine weeks ago. We were supposed to be married the first week in June." Her lower lip trembled a bit. "And then—I got the phone call—they told me—"

A tear rolled down her lovely cheek, and she dabbed at it. Martlett felt uncomfortable. Why, this was almost like paying a call on a new widow! She was in mourning and all.

He said, "I know how you must feel, Miss—ah— Miss Bullard. Michael was a wonderful person—so dynamic, so full of life—"

"And now he's *gone!*" she wailed. "Poof! Vanished off into some other continuum, they told me! Living on some horrible world without air somewhere, maybe!"

"They say it's a quick and painless way to die," Martlett ventured. The words did not soothe her.

The single tear became a torrent; her well-equipped bosom heaved with convulsive sobs. Watching her, Martlett's lips twitched in dismay. Open display of emotion had always been a tribulation for him to witness. He himself felt grief at his brother's passing, certainly, but he had never given way to—to this—

But the sobbing became contagious. "I loved him,"

she moaned. "And he's gone! Gone!" She groped out blindly, fumbled her way onto his shoulder, and let her emotions go. Martlett felt his eyes growing misty at the thought of this girl who had built her whole life around his undeniably remarkable brother, and who now faced nothing but emptiness. Before he knew it, he was crying too.

They sobbed on each other's shoulders for a few moments; then, the fit passing, they straightened up and looked at each other. Her grey eyes were red-rimmed.

"You're so much like him," she murmured. "So tall, so handsome, so—*understanding*."

He felt his face reddening, and nervously moistened his lips. The grief had seemed to fade from her features, and now some other emotion took its place—an emotion Martlett, in thirty years of bachelorhood, had come to recognize with an expert's skill.

Disengaging himself from her, he rose. "I'll have to leave you now, Miss Bullard. It's been a difficult day for me, you understand. But I'll try to see you again before I return to Earth. We've both lost someone very dear to us. Good night, Miss Bullard."

"Why don't you call me Sondra."

He smiled uneasily. "Good night—Sondra."

"Good night, Peter."

Martlett slept that night in his brother's bed, which was a palatial triple-size monstrosity with a pink velvet canopy and a soothing built-in tranquilophone. Martlett found the murmuring wordless sounds of the tranquilophone distracting, but there was no way to shut the thing off, and finally he fell asleep despite it. He dreamed odd dreams and woke feeling unrefreshed in the morning.

Michael's robot butler had prepared a meal for him, Martlett discovered. He wondered whether the robot was aware that the person in the house was *not* his master. Probably not; so far as the robot was concerned, the human of the house *looked* like Mr. Martlett, answered to the name, and therefore *was* Mr. Martlett. That he was the wrong Mr. Martlett did not seem to matter. Robot brains were not geared to such niceties.

Martlett ate thoughtfully, taking his meal on the veranda overlooking Michael's private lake. Sweet-smelling morning breezes drifted toward him. Michael had written that "it is springtime all the year round on Marathon," and he had been telling the truth. Although this was the first time Martlett had visited one of the colony worlds, or indeed had left Earth for any reason at all, he found it hard to imagine a planet more lovely than this one. It would almost be a pity, once he had concluded his business here, to have to return to crowded, untidy Earth once again and go back to the weary business of constructing mindless video jingles.

Better, he thought, to stay here in this eternal spring-time—

No.

He shut off the thought promptly. Whatever he did, he did *not* intend to become a colonist on Marathon. His place was on Earth. Let escapists like Michael flee to this Utopian planet; doubtless laziness and indolence triumphed here, and in a few short generations decadence would be rampant.

The butler came slithering out on the veranda, rolling noiselessly on its treads. "There is a phone call for you, master."

"For me? Can I take it out here?"

The robot registered confusion for an instant. "Surely you know that there is no pickup connection out here, Mr. Martlett?"

"Of course. Silly of me to forget that!"

He followed the robot inside and, tugging his dressing gown tight around himself, entered the camera field of the vidphone. There was a woman's face on the screen— a rather attractive face, Martlett observed, blue-eyed and framed in lustrous blonde hair.

"Good morning," he said, in a flat noncommital voice.

"Oh—you look so much like him!"

"Yes. We almost looked like twins," Martlett said, a trifle edgily. "But I was three years his elder."

"You must be Peter, then. He told me so much about you!"

"Did he? How kind of him. May I ask who it is that I am—"

"Didn't he send you my photo?"

Martlett frowned. "Not that I recall—and I'm sure that I *would* recall, if he had. I'm afraid he didn't."

"Strange," the girl said. "He said he was mailing you a tridim of me. I'm Joanne Hastings."

"Pleased to meet you, Miss Hastings," Martlett said blankly, wondering who Joanne Hastings might be.

She furrowed her forehead prettily. "I said, *Joanne Hastings*. You mean Michael didn't tell you *that* either? Obviously he didn't, because you don't seem to recognize my name at all."

An ominous premonition clogged Martlett's throat. In a hushed voice he said, "I'm afraid Michael didn't tell me anything about you, Miss Hastings."

"Call me Joanne. I am—was—Michael's fiancée. We were going to be married in June, you see."

"Oh. Oh, yes. Yes, I see, Miss Hastings. You and he—were going to get married—in June—"

Martlett closed his eyes briefly, and the image of Sondra Bullard wandered unbidden across the inside of his eyelids. Sondra was a brunette. This girl was a blonde. And Michael had been engaged to both of them.

Suddenly Martlett understood many things he had not been cognizant of before. He realized why Michael had abruptly taken that ill-fated journey to Thermopylae. That it had ended tragically was unfortunate, Martlett reflected—but the Deserializer accident *had* saved Michael from a devilishly nasty dilemma, anyway. Both Joanne and Sondra seemed the predatory kind. Had Michael reached Thermopylae safely, they no doubt would have pursued him there—and from there to Mycenae, and from Mycenae to Thebes, and from there to any other world to which he might flee. Poor Michael! Some of Martlett's grief abated. Had Michael lived, he would never have escaped the clutches of the two females to whom he had so inadvisedly pledged his troth.

With tenderness Martlett said, "I understand, Miss Hastings. His death must have been a dreadful blow to you. As it was to all of us, of course; I loved my brother dearly."

Before he had finished his conversation with Joanne Hastings, he found himself accepting a dinner invitation to her ranch eight hundred miles southward, for the next night. She wanted to talk to him about Michael, and it would have been churlish of him to refuse. He tactfully resolved not to mention to her the matter of Michael's *other* fiancée who called in midmorning, while Martlett was busily wading through the backlog of Michael's unpaid bills and scribbling checks on the veranda. He had dealt with about half of them already; the expenditure so far had been nearly twenty-five hundred units. His rough estimate of three thousand altogether had clearly been inaccurate. But Michael's symphonies would bring royalties forever, Martlett told himself consolingly, as he crossed the veranda and headed for the nearest vidphone at the robot's beck.

Sondra was inconsolably lonely, she sobbed to him, and wanted him to visit her for lunch that day. "You reminded me so much of Michael," she confided. "When you were with me last night I almost felt as though *he* were here!"

Obligingly, Martlett chartered a jetcar once again and flew to her villa for lunch. The visit dragged on until evening, and when Marathon's single big golden moon had spiraled into the sky she insisted he stay for dinner as well. He began to sense that getting Michael's bills paid might take longer than he had expected, at this rate.

He succeeded in disentangling himself by midevening, and flew home deep in brooding thought. The girl seemed perfectly willing to accept him as a substitute for Michael. Most remarkable, he thought. True, there was a physical resemblance so great as to be uncanny, considering the difference in their ages, but as far as personality went they were vastly different. Michael had been flamboyant, witty, spectacular and even a trifle sensational; his older brother tended more toward introspection and sobriety, and most of Michael's women had accordingly shown little interest in Peter's existence. But things seemed to be different with Sondra Bullard, Martlett reflected.

And with Joanne Hastings as well, he discovered the following night, when he kept his dinner engagement with her. He had spent the day in conference with a few of Michael's creditors, people who had neglected to present bills to Secretary Jansen and who now hastened to offer them to Peter.

There was a matter of four hundred units for piano repairs, and three hundred more for music paper. A liquor and wine merchant had sold Michael five magnums of champagne, imported from Earth, fifty units apiece. And so on and so on. The tab was mounting; Martlett estimated he had paid out nearly five thousand units to the creditors of his late brother in these two days, and he was a long way from finished. He wondered how long it would be before Michael's estate earned back five thousand units in royalties, not to mention the nine hundred more it had cost him to come out here.

He was in a morbid frame of mind when he reached Joanne Hastings' ranch, but she soon dispelled his mood. She greeted him dressed in a gay and skimpy plasti-spray outfit that belied her recent loss, and there were cocktails waiting on a tray in the sunken living room.

"You *are* so much like Michael," she told him. "You have the same dark eyes, the same untidy hair, the same way of smiling—"

"Thank you," Martlett said uncertainly. He realized such a situation, but he admitted bleakly to himself that he was not Michael, no matter what these strange women seemed to think.

"It's odd Michael didn't tell you he was planning to marry," she said.

"He never confided much in me," Martlett replied. "Not about such matters, anyway."

"June eighth, it would have been." She sighed. "Well, now it's never to be. Mrs. Michael Martlett—you know, I used to spend hours practising signing my name that way! But—well—"

A lump was beginning to form in Martlett's throat. She seemed so poised, so resigned now to Michael's being dead, and yet behind the outward mask he could plainly see how deeply she felt her loss. He said, "I wish there were something I could do for you, Miss Hastings—"

"Joanne."

"Joanne. But I can't bring Michael back, can I?"

"No," she agreed, after a moment's solemn thought. "No, you can't. All that talent lost in a moment! What a waste!"

"Yes," he said sadly. "What a waste."

She moved a bit closer to him on the couch, and he decided it would be impolite to edge away. She said, "You're *so* much like Michael, dear."

Dear? he wondered. What next?

He said, "You're upset, Miss—Joanne. Let me pour you another drink."

"Yes, do." She moved closer still. "And pour one for yourself."

Somehow it was not at all surprising when he discovered she had her arms around him, and was maneuvering toward him in a way that left him no alternative but to kiss her.

In the next few days, Martlett discerned a clear pattern taking shape, and it frightened him. Not a day went by without a call from one or both of Michael's fiancées, inviting him for dinner. And he was too innately polite to be able to decline their offers.

But, as he spent his days paying Michael's bills (the figure had mounted to seven thousand five hundred units now, and still the creditors arrived in fresh troops) and his evenings sipping cocktails with Michael's betrotheds, he realized what was happening. Both girls—each unaware of the other's presence in the scheme of things—had evidently resolved that if they could not have Michael, they very well were going to have Michael's brother. Martlett was an acceptable substitute to them. Each was spinning a web for him, hoping to trap him into the matrimony he had successfully avoided for thirty consecutive years.

The thought frightened him.

He had come to Marathon to bury Michael, not to inherit his fiancées. It had been his plan to settle Michael's financial affairs, not his romantic ones. He fondly expected to return to Earth in a week or two, still a single man. But yet these girls seemed to be pinning their hopes on snaring him. With each passing day they took less care to hide their true intent.

"Do you still insist on going back to Earth when you've tidied up Michael's bills?" Sondra wanted to know.

"My leave was only for two weeks. I—"

"You could tell your employers you weren't coming back. There must be some advertising agency you could work for on Marathon. And we could live in Michael's villa—"

"We?"

She reddened. "Sorry, darling. Slip of the tongue.

Have another martini, Peter. This Denebian vermouth is delightful."

Eight hours later he was a thousand miles away, consuming cognac in Joanne Hastings' marbled atrium. He had put off Sondra's increasingly more urgent proposals with vague delayers and demurs, but now Joanne was saying, "Peter, dear, you aren't *really* going back to Earth, are you?"

"As soon as I've finished what I came here to do," he said as stolidly as he could considering the amount of alcohol he had ingested that day.

"Which was?"

"To tidy up the loose ends of Michael's fabric of existence, so to speak," he said.

Her delicate eyebrows lifted a fraction of a millimeter. "But—*I'm* one of Michael's loose ends, darling!"

Marlett sighed wearily. "Let's not talk about it now, Joanne. Play that tape of Michael's symphony, would you?" By midday of his ninth day on Marathon, Peter Martlett had at last concluded the job of settling the late Michael Martlett's affairs. All the bills were paid, including a three-thousand-unit mortgage payment on Michael's villa; the total damage had been just under fourteen thousand units, which had wiped out Martlett's savings entirely. Michael's banker had given him the comforting news that he could expect an income of from ten to fifteen thousand units annually from Michael's musical compositions; the fame of a composer always increased immediately after his death, and in Michael's case the tragic circumstance was sure to create a Galaxywide demand for his works.

There was merely the matter of Michael's fiancées to be settled before he left.

Martlett's ethical soul recoiled at the thought of ducking out and popping back to Earth via the Deserializer without even a good-bye, but he knew that was the only possible solution. If he risked calling either or both of them that he was leaving, he could be sure they would artfully ply their wiles and see to it that he remained on Marathon a while longer.

Women, he thought sourly. They bait their hooks with emotion and watch us wriggle when we're caught.

If he spoke to them, they would surely be able to make him stay. And if he stayed, the question of matrimony would inevitably come up. And—the premise followed in rigorous logical sequence—one or the other of the girls would suffer disappointment, while he himself would undergo the equally grave loss of his freedom.

He saw clearly why Michael had decided to bolt to Thermopylae. Lucky Michael had vanished en route, though! He had escaped both forever. And, as had happened so often in the past, it was Big Brother who had to stay around to face the music.

He considered the situation a while. The gentlemanly thing to do—well, there *was* no gentlemanly thing to do. He had both of his brother's women on his hands, and all he could do under the circumstances was run, and fast. Better to jilt both than one, he thought; that way neither would learn that there had been a rival for her affections all along.

After due consideration he phoned Secretary Jansen and announced, "I'm finished with the job. Every debt of Michael's has been paid and I've arranged for the disposition of his personal belongings."

"Glad to hear that. We're pleased you could make the trip, and I hope you enjoyed your stay on Marathon."

"Certainly," Martlett replied. "A wonderful planet. But my work on Earth awaits me. How soon can I have accommodations on the outward journey?"

"You're in luck—a ship leaves for Earth at midnight. You can show up any time, as late as eleven, to be deserialized and placed on board."

"I'll be there," Martlett said.

He broke the contact, feeling an abiding sense of guilt. *So I'm a cad, he thought. So what? I didn't ask them to fall in love with me. They aren't in love with me, anyway. Just with Michael's image.*

He was half finished with the task of packing his meager belongings when the phone chime sounded. Activating the controls, he was dismayed to see the blonde tresses of Joanne Hastings in three dimensions and natural color.

"Peter—I hear you're leaving!"

"Where did you get that idea?"

"Don't try to pretend it isn't so! I—I have my sources of information. Peter, darling, why are you going?"

"I told you," he said, trying with only moderate success to put a flinty edge on his voice. "I'm an Earthman, not a colonist. I'm going home."

"Then I'll go with you! Darling, wait for me! Take me to Earth—I'll be your slave! I'm leaving now. I'll be at your villa in half an hour. Don't refuse me, Peter. I can't bear to lose you."

Martlett goggled and tried to reply, but before words would come out she had blanked the screen. He stared blearily at the sleek surface of the dead screen a moment, stunned. Coming here? In half an hour? But—

The phone chimed again.

With numbed fingers he activated it and watched the features of Sondra Bullard come swirling out of the electronic haze. She had heard he was leaving, she told him, and she implored him to change his mind. "Don't go," she begged him. "Stay right where you are. I'm on my way now. I have to see you again in person. I'll be there in half an hour. I love you, Peter."

"Half an hour? Aiee! Sondra—"

Too late. The screen was dead again.

Martlett remained quite still, sorting out the rush of thoughts that rippled through his chilled mind. They had both heard that he was leaving; that meant that most likely both, anticipating another runout à la Michael, had arranged with some underling of the secretary to be notified the moment he announced his intention to depart.

And they were on their way here to persuade him to change his mind. Joanne would be here in half an hour. Sondra would be here in half an hour. That meant—

He knew what that meant. They would *both* be here in half an hour. They were travelling on a collision orbit. And when they got together, critical mass would be reached rapidly.

Well, he thought in desperation, there was a clear path to safety still. All he had to do was report to the deserializing office *now*, and have them tuck him away in the Henderson Field until the midnight departure time. So far as it would matter to him, the elapsed time would be the same—hardly any at all—and he would be safely out of the reach of those grasping altar-eager females.

Martlett smiled. Yes, he thought. That's what I'll do!

He ordered the butler to get the jetcar ready for an immediate trip downtown. And in the meanwhile, he thought, there still is time for a drink. Something to calm my nerves. I paid two thousand units to settle Michael's liquor bills; I might as well enjoy some of it.

There was a liquor cabinet and dial bar at the opposite end of the living room. Martlett half skipped to it and quickly punched out an order for a double bourbon. Nothing happened; and then he recalled he had ordered the bar fixture disconnected that morning.

Shrugging, he tugged open the panelled door of the liquor cabinet and groped inside for one of the bottles. It was dim and dusty in there; he fumbled for a handhold, finally catching something—

He pulled.

What came out was not a bottle. He had been grasping a lever attached to a square black enamel box, and now box and lever both came out of the cabinet suddenly. He let go of the lever and jumped back. The box had popped open. "Damn," an oddly familiar voice said. "So soon?"

The box expanded abruptly. Martlett edged further back, and in the same moment a man stepped out of the box, stretching as if he had been crouching on his knees a long while and at last was standing up. He was tall— about Martlett's own height. He had unruly brown hair and a roguish smile, and a fine network of laugh wrinkles around his eyes.

He might almost have been Martlett's twin. He was, in point of fact, his younger brother.

He chuckled amiably and said, "Well, Peter—you're the last person I expected to see at this moment!"

Martlett backed up feebly. "Michael! You're—alive?"

"Extremely, dear brother. Would you mind telling me what year this is?"

Weakly, Martlett said, "2209. April 20th."

"Ha! The little vixens! Not even two months, and they've forgotten me already! Pfoo, it's dusty in here! What are *you* doing on Marathon, old man?"

In a chilly voice Martlett said, "After you were pronounced legally dead I was called here to serve as executor of your estate, Michael. I paid out some fourteen thousand units you owed. And now to find you're still alive! What—how—"

"I dare say you think it's ungrateful of me to come back to life, eh?" Michael smiled cozily. "Well, it was good of you to take care of the debts, Peter. This job did cost me a penny or two, and I'm afraid I rather neglected the tradesmen the while."

"What job? What are you talking about?"

"Why, the private Deserializer I had built, of course!"

Martlett put his hands to his head. He felt close to madness; the sudden arrival of his brother, the importuning of those girls, the fourteen thousand units, all seemed to swirl wildly around him. In a dark voice he said, "Will you explain yourself, Michael?"

"Certainly. There were these girls, you see—Joanne

was the blonde, and Sandra the brunette."

"Yes, I know."

"Lovely, weren't they? Anyhow, with my usual care-lessness I contrived to get myself engaged to both of them. It was an awkward situation; they both vowed to follow me to the ends of the universe, et cetera, the usual stuff. Damned tenacious lasses, both."

"I know that too," Martlett said.

"Do you, now? Well, to make the matter short," said Michael, "I found it expedient to disappear. I hired a person to arrange things for me, at a fee. He caused it to seem as if I had vanished in some awful way en route to Thermopylae or some such place in this system, when actually I hadn't even made the trip! I was deserialized and locked away in my own liquor closet, y'see, in cold storage, not conscious of the passage of time. There was a timer on the thing which would release me in five objective years—but you surely must know all about this?"

"On the contrary. It's quite new to me."

"But the arrangement was that my fellow would keep an eye on those two girls, and if they both got married before the five years were up he'd come around to let me out of the deserializer field right away. And since you've released me, then obviously—"

"No," Martlett said. "I pulled you out of the closet by accident. I thought you were dead."

"But I was only in there two months. And the girls—?"

"Still single. Both of them."

Michael's face turned paper white and he nibbled at his lips. "You mean they're both on the loose and you've released me. Oh, Peter, you incorrigible bungler! You—"

"Worse than that," Martlett interrupted. "They're both on their way here right now. They've decided to marry me, as long as you weren't available. They'll be here

in—" he consulted his watch—"about four minutes, unless they happen to arrive early."

Michael was galvanized suddenly into frantic exer-
tion. "Quick, then! I've got to leave here! If they ever
find me alive they'll rip me to shreds!"

The butler suddenly rolled into the living room. It
darted a confused glance from one Martlett brother to
the other, and, its gears meshing and clanking in bewil-
derment, it announced, "Two ladies have just arrived to
see Mr. Martlett."

"Tell them I'm not home!" Martlett and his brother
shouted simultaneously.

"They insist on entering," the robot said.

Michael clutched at his brother's sleeve in panic. "What
will we do?"

The outer doors were opening. The sound of agitated
feminine conversation was audible outside. "Don't let
them in," Michael ordered the butler. But the shock of
seeing duplicate masters had put the robot out of com-
mission; it drooled quietly to itself without obeying.

Martlett said in a voice heavy with defeat. "I guess
we'll have to marry them, I suppose. Explain things
first—we'll say you miraculously popped back into the
continuum—and then marry them. We can't escape, Michael. And we *could* do worse for women, you know."

The voices were coming closer. "I guess you're right,"
Michael said. Lines of strain showed on his boyish face.
"But—good grief, Peter!—*who marries which one?*"

Martlett shrugged. "Does it matter? I suppose we can
toss for it."

Sounds reached them: *"Peter, darling, are you in
there?"* And *"Who is this horrible woman, Peter?"*

Peter looked at his brother. It was the first time he
had ever seen Michael actually quaking with fear. "Stiff
upper lip, boy," he muttered. "It shouldn't be so bad
once you've explained."

"You explain," Michael said. "I don't dare."

"You'd better dare," Peter retorted. "You got us into this in the first place. You and your private Deserializer."

And there was no getting out, he thought, looking toward the door through which the girls were about to burst. They were trapped for fair. Might as well make the best of it.

Shoulder to shoulder, the Martlett brothers stood their ground and waited resignedly for the enemy to storm the battlements.

MORE SCIENCE FICTION ADVENTURE!

BESTSELLING
Science Fiction
and
Fantasy

ROBERT A. HEINLEIN
THE MODERN MASTER OF SCIENCE FICTION

___ FARNHAM'S FREEHOLD   (08379-9 — $3.50)

___ GLORY ROAD   (08898-7 — $3.50)

___ I WILL FEAR NO EVIL   (08680-1 — $3.95)

___ THE MOON IS A
      HARSH MISTRESS   (08100-1 — $3.50)

___ ORPHANS OF THE SKY   (08225-3 — $2.75)

___ THE PAST THROUGH
      TOMORROW   (06458-1 — $3.95)

___ PODKAYNE OF MARS   (08901-0 — $2.95)

___ STARSHIP TROOPERS   (07158-8 — $2.75)

___ STRANGER
      IN A STRANGE LAND   (08094-3 — $3.95)

___ TIME ENOUGH FOR LOVE   (07050-6 — $3.95)

___ TOMORROW THE STARS   (07572-9 — $2.75)

Prices may be slightly higher in Canada.

Available at your local bookstore or return this form to:

 BERKLEY
Book Mailing Service
P.O. Box 690, Rockville Centre, NY 11571

Please send me the titles checked above. I enclose _____ Include 75¢ for postage and handling if one book is ordered; 25¢ per book for two or more not to exceed $1.75. California, Illinois, New York and Tennessee residents please add sales tax.

NAME _____

ADDRESS _____

CITY _____ STATE/ZIP _____

(allow six weeks for delivery)   **75J**